Epicoene

Or, The Silent Woman

Ben Jonson

Epicoene; Or, The Silent Woman

The present edition is a reproduction of previous publication of this classic work. Minor typographical errors may have been corrected without note; however, for an authentic reading experience the spelling, punctuation, and capitalization have been retained from the original text.

ISBN: 978-1-64799-657-4

CONTENTS

INTRODUCTION

THE greatest of English dramatists except Shakespeare, the first literary dictator and poet-laureate, a writer of verse, prose, satire, and criticism who most potently of all the men of his time affected the subsequent course of English letters: such was Ben Jonson, and as such his strong personality assumes an interest to us almost unparalleled, at least in his age.

Ben Jonson came of the stock that was centuries after to give to the world Thomas Carlyle; for Jonson's grandfather was of Annandale, over the Solway, whence he migrated to England. Jonson's father lost his estate under Queen Mary, "having been cast into prison and forfeited." He entered the church, but died a month before his illustrious son was born, leaving his widow and child in poverty. Jonson's birthplace was Westminster, and the time of his birth early in 1573. He was thus nearly ten years Shakespeare's junior, and less well off, if a trifle better born. But Jonson did not profit even by this slight advantage. His mother married beneath her, a wright or bricklayer, and Jonson was for a time apprenticed to the trade. As a youth he attracted the attention of the famous antiquary, William Camden, then usher at Westminster School, and there the poet laid the solid foundations of his classical learning. Jonson always held Camden in veneration, acknowledging that to him he owed,

"All that I am in arts, all that I know;"

and dedicating his first dramatic success, "Every Man in His Humour," to him. It is doubtful whether Jonson ever went to either university, though Fuller says that he was "statutably admitted into St. John's College, Cambridge." He tells us that he took no degree, but was later "Master of Arts in both the universities, by their favour, not his study." When a mere youth Jonson enlisted as a soldier, trailing his pike in Flanders in the protracted wars of William the Silent against the Spanish. Jonson was a large and raw-boned lad; he became by his own account in time exceedingly bulky. In chat with his friend William Drummond of Hawthornden, Jonson told how "in his service in the Low Countries he had, in the face of both the camps, killed an enemy, and taken opima spolia from him;" and how "since his coming to England, being appealed to the fields, he had killed his adversary which had hurt him in the arm and whose sword was ten inches longer than his." Jonson's reach may have made up for the lack of his sword; certainly his prowess lost nothing in the telling. Obviously Jonson was brave, combative, and not averse to talking of himself and his doings.

In 1592, Jonson returned from abroad penniless. Soon after he married, almost as early and quite as imprudently as Shakespeare. He told Drummond curtly that "his wife was a shrew, yet honest"; for some years he lived apart from her in the household of Lord Albany. Yet two touching epitaphs among Jonson's "Epigrams," "On my first daughter," and "On my first son," attest the warmth of the poet's family affections. The daughter died in infancy, the son of the plague; another son grew up to manhood little credit to his father whom he survived. We know nothing beyond this of Jonson's domestic life.

How soon Jonson drifted into what we now call grandly "the theatrical profession" we do not know. In 1593, Marlowe made his tragic exit from life, and Greene, Shakespeare's other rival on the popular stage, had preceded Marlowe in an equally miserable death the year before. Shakespeare already had the running to himself. Jonson appears first in the employment of Philip Henslowe, the exploiter of several troupes of players, manager, and father-in-law of the famous actor, Edward Alleyn. From entries in "Henslowe's Diary," a species of theatrical account book which has been handed down to us, we know that Jonson was connected with the Admiral's men; for he borrowed 4 pounds of Henslowe, July 28, 1597, paying back 3s. 9d. on the same day on account of his "share" (in what is not altogether clear); while later, on December 3, of the same year, Henslowe advanced 20s. to him "upon a book which he showed the plot unto the company which he promised to deliver unto the company at Christmas next." In the next August Jonson was in collaboration with Chettle and Porter in a play called "Hot Anger Soon Cold." All this points to an association with Henslowe of some duration, as no mere tyro would be thus paid in advance upon mere promise. From allusions in Dekker's play, "Satiromastix," it appears that Jonson, like Shakespeare, began life as an actor, and that he "ambled in a leather pitch by a play-wagon" taking at one time the part of Hieronimo in Kyd's famous play, "The Spanish Tragedy." By the beginning of 1598, Jonson, though still in needy circumstances, had begun to receive recognition. Francis Meres — well known for his "Comparative Discourse of our English Poets with the Greek, Latin, and Italian Poets," printed in 1598, and for his mention therein of a dozen plays of Shakespeare by title — accords to Ben Jonson a place as one of "our best in tragedy," a matter of some surprise, as no known tragedy of Jonson from so early a date has come down to us. That Jonson was at work on tragedy, however, is proved by the entries in Henslowe of at least three tragedies, now lost, in which he had a hand. These are "Page of Plymouth," "King Robert II. of Scotland," and "Richard Crookback." But all of these came later, on his return to Henslowe, and range from August 1599 to June 1602.

Returning to the autumn of 1598, an event now happened to sever for a time Jonson's relations with Henslowe. In a letter to Alleyn, dated September 26 of that year, Henslowe writes: "I have lost one of my company that hurteth me greatly; that is Gabriel [Spencer], for he is slain in Hogsden fields by the hands of Benjamin Jonson, bricklayer." The last word is perhaps Henslowe's thrust at Jonson in his displeasure rather than a designation of his actual continuance at his trade up to this time. It is fair to Jonson to remark however, that his adversary appears to have been a notorious fire-eater who had shortly before killed one Feeke in a similar squabble. Duelling was a frequent occurrence of the time among gentlemen and the nobility; it was an impudent breach of the peace on the part of a player. This duel is the one which Jonson described years after to Drummond, and for it Jonson was duly arraigned at Old Bailey, tried, and convicted. He was sent to prison and such goods and chattels as he had "were forfeited." It is a thought to give one pause that, but for the ancient law permitting convicted felons to plead, as it was called, the benefit of clergy, Jonson might have been hanged for this deed. The circumstance that the poet could read and write saved him; and he received only a brand of the letter "T," for Tyburn, on his left thumb. While in jail Jonson became a Roman Catholic; but he returned to the faith of the Church of England a dozen years later.

On his release, in disgrace with Henslowe and his former associates, Jonson offered his services as a playwright to Henslowe's rivals, the Lord Chamberlain's company, in which Shakespeare was a prominent shareholder. A tradition of long standing, though not susceptible of proof in a court of law, narrates that Jonson had submitted the manuscript of "Every Man in His Humour" to the Chamberlain's men and had received from the company a refusal; that Shakespeare called him back, read the play himself, and at once accepted it. Whether this story is true or not, certain it is that "Every Man in His Humour" was accepted by Shakespeare's company and acted for the first time in 1598, with Shakespeare taking a part. The evidence of this is contained in the list of actors prefixed to the comedy in the folio of Jonson's works, 1616. But it is a mistake to infer, because Shakespeare's name stands first in the list of actors and the elder Kno'well first in the dramatis personae, that Shakespeare took that particular part. The order of a list of Elizabethan players was generally that of their importance or priority as shareholders in the company and seldom if ever corresponded to the list of characters.

"Every Man in His Humour" was an immediate success, and with it Jonson's reputation as one of the leading dramatists of his time was established once and for all. This could have been by no means Jonson's earliest comedy, and we have just learned that he was already reputed one of "our best in tragedy." Indeed, one of Jonson's extant comedies, "The Case is Altered," but one never claimed by him or published as his, must certainly have preceded "Every Man in His Humour" on the stage. The former play may be described as a comedy modelled on the Latin plays of Plautus. (It combines, in fact, situations derived from the "Captivi" and the "Aulularia" of that dramatist). But the pretty story of the beggar-maiden, Rachel, and her suitors, Jonson found, not among the classics, but in the ideals of romantic love which Shakespeare had already popularised on the stage. Jonson never again produced so fresh and lovable a feminine personage as Rachel, although in other respects "The Case is Altered" is not a conspicuous play, and, save for the satirising of Antony Munday in the person of Antonio Balladino and Gabriel Harvey as well, is perhaps the least characteristic of the comedies of Jonson.

"Every Man in His Humour," probably first acted late in the summer of 1598 and at the Curtain, is commonly regarded as an epoch-making play; and this view is not unjustified. As to plot, it tells little more than how an intercepted letter enabled a father to follow his supposedly studious son to London, and there observe his life with the gallants of the time. The real quality of this comedy is in its personages and in the theory upon which they are conceived. Ben Jonson had theories about poetry and the drama, and he was neither chary in talking of them nor in experimenting with them in his plays. This makes Jonson, like Dryden in his time, and Wordsworth much later, an author to reckon with; particularly when we remember that many of Jonson's notions came for a time definitely to prevail and to modify the whole trend of English poetry. First of all Jonson was a classicist, that is, he believed in restraint and precedent in art in opposition to the prevalent ungoverned and irresponsible Renaissance spirit. Jonson believed that there was a professional way of doing things which might be reached by a study of the best examples, and he found these examples for the most part among the ancients. To confine our attention to the drama, Jonson objected to the amateurishness and haphazard nature of many contemporary plays, and set himself to do something different; and the first and most striking thing that he evolved was his conception and practice of the comedy of humours.

As Jonson has been much misrepresented in this matter, let us quote his own words as to "humour." A humour, according to Jonson, was a bias of disposition, a warp, so to speak, in character by which

> *"Some one peculiar quality*
> *Doth so possess a man, that it doth draw*
> *All his affects, his spirits, and his powers,*
> *In their confluctions, all to run one way."*

But continuing, Jonson is careful to add:

> *"But that a rook by wearing a pied feather,*
> *The cable hat-band, or the three-piled ruff,*
> *A yard of shoe-tie, or the Switzers knot*
> *On his French garters, should affect a humour!*
> *O, it is more than most ridiculous."*

Jonson's comedy of humours, in a word, conceived of stage personages on the basis of a ruling trait or passion (a notable simplification of actual life be it observed in passing); and, placing these typified traits in juxtaposition in their conflict and contrast, struck the spark of comedy. Downright, as his name indicates, is "a plain squire"; Bobadill's humour is that of the braggart who is incidentally, and with delightfully comic effect, a coward; Brainworm's humour is the finding out of things to the end of fooling everybody: of course he is fooled in the end himself. But it was not Jonson's theories alone that made the success of "Every Man in His Humour." The play is admirably written and each character is vividly conceived, and with a firm touch based on observation of the men of the London of the day. Jonson was neither in this, his first great comedy (nor in any other play that he wrote), a supine classicist, urging that English drama return to a slavish adherence to classical conditions. He says as to the laws of the old comedy (meaning by "laws," such matters as the unities of time and place and the use of chorus): "I see not then, but we should enjoy the same licence, or free power to illustrate and heighten our invention as they [the ancients] did; and not be tied to those strict and regular forms which the niceness of a few, who are nothing but form, would thrust upon us." "Every Man in His Humour" is written in prose, a novel practice which Jonson had of his predecessor in comedy, John Lyly. Even the word "humour" seems to have been employed in the Jonsonian sense by Chapman before Jonson's use of it. Indeed, the comedy of humours itself is only a heightened variety of the comedy of manners which represents life, viewed at a satirical angle, and is the oldest and most persistent species of comedy in the language. None the less, Jonson's comedy merited its immediate success and marked out a definite course in which comedy long continued to run. To mention only Shakespeare's Falstaff and his rout, Bardolph, Pistol, Dame Quickly, and the rest, whether in "Henry IV." or in "The Merry Wives of Windsor," all are conceived in the spirit of humours. So are the captains, Welsh, Scotch, and Irish of "Henry V.," and Malvolio especially later; though Shakespeare never employed the method of humours for an important personage. It was not Jonson's fault that many of his successors did precisely the thing that he had reprobated, that is, degrade the humour: into an oddity of speech, an eccentricity of manner, of dress, or cut of beard. There was an anonymous play called "Every Woman in Her Humour." Chapman wrote "A Humourous Day's Mirth," Day, "Humour Out of Breath," Fletcher later, "The Humourous Lieutenant," and Jonson, besides "Every Man Out of His Humour," returned to the title in closing the cycle of his comedies in "The Magnetic Lady or Humours Reconciled."

With the performance of "Every Man Out of His Humour" in 1599, by Shakespeare's company once more at the Globe, we turn a new page in Jonson's career. Despite his many real virtues, if there is one feature more than any other that distinguishes Jonson, it is his arrogance; and to this may be added his self-righteousness, especially under criticism or satire. "Every Man Out of His Humour" is the first of three "comical satires" which Jonson contributed to what Dekker called the poetomachia or war of the theatres as recent critics have named it. This play as a fabric of plot is a very slight affair; but as a satirical picture of the manners of the time, proceeding by means of vivid caricature, couched in witty and brilliant dialogue and sustained by that righteous indignation which must lie at the heart of all true satire — as a realisation, in short, of the classical ideal of comedy — there had been nothing like Jonson's comedy since the days of Aristophanes. "Every Man in His Humour," like the two plays that follow it, contains two kinds of attack, the critical or generally satiric, levelled at abuses and corruptions in the abstract; and the personal, in which specific application is made of all this in the lampooning of poets and others, Jonson's contemporaries. The method of personal attack by actual caricature of a person on the stage is almost as old as the drama. Aristophanes so lampooned Euripides in "The Acharnians" and Socrates in "The Clouds," to mention no other examples; and in English drama this kind of thing is alluded to again and again. What Jonson really did, was to raise the dramatic lampoon to an art, and make out of a casual burlesque and bit of mimicry a dramatic satire of literary pretensions and permanency. With the arrogant attitude mentioned above and his uncommon eloquence in scorn, vituperation, and invective, it is no wonder that Jonson soon involved himself in literary and even personal quarrels with his fellow-authors. The circumstances of the origin of this 'poetomachia' are far from clear, and those who have written on the topic, except of late, have not helped to make them clearer. The origin of the "war" has been referred to satirical references, apparently to Jonson, contained in "The Scourge of Villainy," a satire in regular form after the manner of the ancients by John Marston, a fellow playwright, subsequent friend and collaborator of Jonson's. On the other hand, epigrams of Jonson have been discovered (49, 68, and 100) variously charging "playwright" (reasonably identified with Marston) with scurrility, cowardice, and plagiarism; though the dates of the epigrams cannot be ascertained with certainty. Jonson's own statement of the matter to Drummond runs: "He had many quarrels with Marston, beat him, and took his pistol from him, wrote his "Poetaster" on him; the beginning[s] of them were that Marston represented him on the stage."[1]

Here at least we are on certain ground; and the principals of the quarrel are known. "Histriomastix," a play revised by Marston in 1598, has been regarded as the one in which Jonson was thus "represented on the stage"; although the personage in question, Chrisogonus, a poet, satirist, and translator, poor but proud, and contemptuous of the common herd, seems rather a complimentary portrait of Jonson than a caricature. As to the personages actually ridiculed in "Every Man Out of His Humour," Carlo Buffone was formerly thought certainly to be Marston, as he was described as "a public, scurrilous, and profane jester," and elsewhere as the grand scourge or second untruss [that is, satirist], of the time (Joseph Hall being by his own boast the first, and Marston's work being entitled "The Scourge of Villainy"). Apparently we must now prefer for Carlo a notorious character named Charles Chester, of whom gossipy and inaccurate Aubrey relates that he was "a bold impertinent fellow...a perpetual talker and made a noise like a drum in a room. So one time at a tavern Sir Walter Raleigh beats him and seals up his mouth (that is his upper and nether beard) with hard wax. From him Ben Jonson takes his Carlo Buffone ['i.e.', jester] in "Every Man in His Humour" ['sic']." Is it conceivable that after all Jonson was

---

[1] The best account of this whole subject is to be found in the edition of "Poetaster" and "Satiromastix" by J. H. Penniman in "Belles Lettres Series" shortly to appear. See also his earlier work, "The War of the Theatres," 1892, and the excellent contributions to the subject by H. C. Hart in "Notes and Queries," and in his edition of Jonson, 1906.

ridiculing Marston, and that the point of the satire consisted in an intentional confusion of "the grand scourge or second untruss" with "the scurrilous and profane" Chester?

We have digressed into detail in this particular case to exemplify the difficulties of criticism in its attempts to identify the allusions in these forgotten quarrels. We are on sounder ground of fact in recording other manifestations of Jonson's enmity. In "The Case is Altered" there is clear ridicule in the character Antonio Balladino of Anthony Munday, pageant-poet of the city, translator of romances and playwright as well. In "Every Man in His Humour" there is certainly a caricature of Samuel Daniel, accepted poet of the court, sonneteer, and companion of men of fashion. These men held recognised positions to which Jonson felt his talents better entitled him; they were hence to him his natural enemies. It seems almost certain that he pursued both in the personages of his satire through "Every Man Out of His Humour," and "Cynthia's Revels," Daniel under the characters Fastidious Brisk and Hedon, Munday as Puntarvolo and Amorphus; but in these last we venture on quagmire once more. Jonson's literary rivalry of Daniel is traceable again and again, in the entertainments that welcomed King James on his way to London, in the masques at court, and in the pastoral drama. As to Jonson's personal ambitions with respect to these two men, it is notable that he became, not pageant-poet, but chronologer to the City of London; and that, on the accession of the new king, he came soon to triumph over Daniel as the accepted entertainer of royalty.

"Cynthia's Revels," the second "comical satire," was acted in 1600, and, as a play, is even more lengthy, elaborate, and impossible than "Every Man Out of His Humour." Here personal satire seems to have absorbed everything, and while much of the caricature is admirable, especially in the detail of witty and trenchantly satirical dialogue, the central idea of a fountain of self-love is not very well carried out, and the persons revert at times to abstractions, the action to allegory. It adds to our wonder that this difficult drama should have been acted by the Children of Queen Elizabeth's Chapel, among them Nathaniel Field with whom Jonson read Horace and Martial, and whom he taught later how to make plays. Another of these precocious little actors was Salathiel Pavy, who died before he was thirteen, already famed for taking the parts of old men. Him Jonson immortalised in one of the sweetest of his epitaphs. An interesting sidelight is this on the character of this redoubtable and rugged satirist, that he should thus have befriended and tenderly remembered these little theatrical waifs, some of whom (as we know) had been literally kidnapped to be pressed into the service of the theatre and whipped to the conning of their difficult parts. To the caricature of Daniel and Munday in "Cynthia's Revels" must be added Anaides (impudence), here assuredly Marston, and Asotus (the prodigal), interpreted as Lodge or, more perilously, Raleigh. Crites, like Asper-Macilente in "Every Man Out of His Humour," is Jonson's self-complaisant portrait of himself, the just, wholly admirable, and judicious scholar, holding his head high above the pack of the yelping curs of envy and detraction, but careless of their puny attacks on his perfections with only too mindful a neglect.

The third and last of the "comical satires" is "Poetaster," acted, once more, by the Children of the Chapel in 1601, and Jonson's only avowed contribution to the fray. According to the author's own account, this play was written in fifteen weeks on a report that his enemies had entrusted to Dekker the preparation of "Satiromastix, the Untrussing of the Humorous Poet," a dramatic attack upon himself. In this attempt to forestall his enemies Jonson succeeded, and "Poetaster" was an immediate and deserved success. While hardly more closely knit in structure than its earlier companion pieces, "Poetaster" is planned to lead up to the ludicrous final scene in which, after a device borrowed from the "Lexiphanes" of Lucian, the offending poetaster, Marston-Crispinus, is made to throw up the difficult words with which he had overburdened his stomach as well as overlarded his vocabulary. In the end Crispinus with his fellow, Dekker-Demetrius, is bound over to keep the peace and never thenceforward "malign, traduce, or detract the person or writings of Quintus Horatius Flaccus [Jonson] or any other eminent man transcending you in merit." One of the most diverting personages in Jonson's comedy is Captain Tucca. "His peculiarity" has been well described by Ward as "a buoyant blackguardism which recovers itself instantaneously from the most complete exposure, and a picturesqueness of speech like that of a walking dictionary of slang."

It was this character, Captain Tucca, that Dekker hit upon in his reply, "Satiromastix," and he amplified him, turning his abusive vocabulary back upon Jonson and adding "an immodesty to his dialogue that did not enter into Jonson's conception." It has been held, altogether plausibly, that when Dekker was engaged professionally, so to speak, to write a dramatic reply to Jonson, he was at work on a species of chronicle history, dealing with the story of Walter Terill in the reign of William Rufus. This he hurriedly adapted to include the satirical characters suggested by "Poetaster," and fashioned to convey the satire of his reply. The absurdity of placing Horace in the court of a Norman king is the result. But

Dekker's play is not without its palpable hits at the arrogance, the literary pride, and self-righteousness of Jonson-Horace, whose "ningle" or pal, the absurd Asinius Bubo, has recently been shown to figure forth, in all likelihood, Jonson's friend, the poet Drayton. Slight and hastily adapted as is "Satiromastix," especially in a comparison with the better wrought and more significant satire of "Poetaster," the town awarded the palm to Dekker, not to Jonson; and Jonson gave over in consequence his practice of "comical satire." Though Jonson was cited to appear before the Lord Chief Justice to answer certain charges to the effect that he had attacked lawyers and soldiers in "Poetaster," nothing came of this complaint. It may be suspected that much of this furious clatter and give-and-take was pure playing to the gallery. The town was agog with the strife, and on no less an authority than Shakespeare ("Hamlet," ii. 2), we learn that the children's company (acting the plays of Jonson) did "so berattle the common stages...that many, wearing rapiers, are afraid of goose-quills, and dare scarce come thither."

Several other plays have been thought to bear a greater or less part in the war of the theatres. Among them the most important is a college play, entitled "The Return from Parnassus," dating 1601-02. In it a much-quoted passage makes Burbage, as a character, declare: "Why here's our fellow Shakespeare puts them all down; aye and Ben Jonson, too. O that Ben Jonson is a pestilent fellow; he brought up Horace, giving the poets a pill, but our fellow Shakespeare hath given him a purge that made him bewray his credit." Was Shakespeare then concerned in this war of the stages? And what could have been the nature of this "purge"? Among several suggestions, "Troilus and Cressida" has been thought by some to be the play in which Shakespeare thus "put down" his friend, Jonson. A wiser interpretation finds the "purge" in "Satiromastix," which, though not written by Shakespeare, was staged by his company, and therefore with his approval and under his direction as one of the leaders of that company.

The last years of the reign of Elizabeth thus saw Jonson recognised as a dramatist second only to Shakespeare, and not second even to him as a dramatic satirist. But Jonson now turned his talents to new fields. Plays on subjects derived from classical story and myth had held the stage from the beginning of the drama, so that Shakespeare was making no new departure when he wrote his "Julius Caesar" about 1600. Therefore when Jonson staged "Sejanus," three years later and with Shakespeare's company once more, he was only following in the elder dramatist's footsteps. But Jonson's idea of a play on classical history, on the one hand, and Shakespeare's and the elder popular dramatists, on the other, were very different. Heywood some years before had put five straggling plays on the stage in quick succession, all derived from stories in Ovid and dramatised with little taste or discrimination. Shakespeare had a finer conception of form, but even he was contented to take all his ancient history from North's translation of Plutarch and dramatise his subject without further inquiry. Jonson was a scholar and a classical antiquarian. He reprobated this slipshod amateurishness, and wrote his "Sejanus" like a scholar, reading Tacitus, Suetonius, and other authorities, to be certain of his facts, his setting, and his atmosphere, and somewhat pedantically noting his authorities in the margin when he came to print. "Sejanus" is a tragedy of genuine dramatic power in which is told with discriminating taste the story of the haughty favourite of Tiberius with his tragical overthrow. Our drama presents no truer nor more painstaking representation of ancient Roman life than may be found in Jonson's "Sejanus" and "Catiline his Conspiracy," which followed in 1611. A passage in the address of the former play to the reader, in which Jonson refers to a collaboration in an earlier version, has led to the surmise that Shakespeare may have been that "worthier pen." There is no evidence to determine the matter.

In 1605, we find Jonson in active collaboration with Chapman and Marston in the admirable comedy of London life entitled "Eastward Hoe." In the previous year, Marston had dedicated his "Malcontent," in terms of fervid admiration, to Jonson; so that the wounds of the war of the theatres must have been long since healed. Between Jonson and Chapman there was the kinship of similar scholarly ideals. The two continued friends throughout life. "Eastward Hoe" achieved the extraordinary popularity represented in a demand for three issues in one year. But this was not due entirely to the merits of the play. In its earliest version a passage which an irritable courtier conceived to be derogatory to his nation, the Scots, sent both Chapman and Jonson to jail; but the matter was soon patched up, for by this time Jonson had influence at court.

With the accession of King James, Jonson began his long and successful career as a writer of masques. He wrote more masques than all his competitors together, and they are of an extraordinary variety and poetic excellence. Jonson did not invent the masque; for such premeditated devices to set and frame, so to speak, a court ball had been known and practised in varying degrees of elaboration long before his time. But Jonson gave dramatic value to the masque, especially in his invention of the antimasque, a comedy or farcical element of relief, entrusted to professional players or dancers. He enhanced, as well, the beauty and dignity of those portions of the masque in which noble lords and ladies took their parts to create, by their gorgeous costumes and artistic grouping and evolutions, a sumptuous show. On the mechanical and scenic side Jonson had an inventive and ingenious partner in Inigo Jones, the royal architect, who more than any one man raised the standard of stage representation in the England of his day. Jonson continued active in the service of the court in the writing of masques and other entertainments far into the reign of King Charles; but, towards the end, a quarrel with Jones embittered his life, and the two testy old men appear to have become not only a constant irritation to each other, but intolerable bores at court. In "Hymenaei," "The Masque of Queens," "Love Freed from Ignorance," "Lovers made Men," "Pleasure Reconciled to Virtue," and many more will be found Jonson's aptitude, his taste, his poetry and inventiveness in these by-forms of the drama; while in "The Masque of Christmas," and "The Gipsies Metamorphosed" especially, is discoverable that power of broad comedy which, at court as well as in the city, was not the least element of Jonson's contemporary popularity.

But Jonson had by no means given up the popular stage when he turned to the amusement of King James. In 1605 "Volpone" was produced, "The Silent Woman" in 1609, "The Alchemist" in the following year. These comedies, with "Bartholomew Fair," 1614, represent Jonson at his height, and for constructive cleverness, character successfully conceived in the manner of caricature, wit and brilliancy of dialogue, they stand alone in English drama. "Volpone, or the Fox," is, in a sense, a transition play from the dramatic satires of the war of the theatres to the purer comedy represented in the plays named above. Its subject is a struggle of wit applied to chicanery; for among its dramatis personae, from the villainous Fox himself, his rascally servant Mosca, Voltore (the vulture), Corbaccio and Corvino (the big and the little raven), to Sir Politic Would-be and the rest, there is scarcely a virtuous character in the play. Question has been raised as to whether a story so forbidding can be considered a comedy, for, although the plot ends in the discomfiture and imprisonment of the most vicious, it involves no mortal catastrophe. But Jonson was on sound historical ground, for "Volpone" is conceived far more logically on the lines of the ancients' theory of comedy than was ever the romantic drama of Shakespeare, however repulsive we may find a philosophy of life that facilely divides the world into the rogues and their dupes, and, identifying brains with roguery and innocence with folly, admires the former while inconsistently punishing them.

"The Silent Woman" is a gigantic farce of the most ingenious construction. The whole comedy hinges on a huge joke, played by a heartless nephew on his misanthropic uncle, who is induced to take to himself a wife, young, fair, and warranted silent, but who, in the end, turns out neither silent nor a woman at all. In "The Alchemist," again, we have the utmost cleverness in construction, the whole fabric building climax on climax, witty, ingenious, and so plausibly presented that we forget its departures from the possibilities of life. In "The Alchemist" Jonson represented, none the less to the life, certain sharpers of the metropolis, revelling in their shrewdness and rascality and in the variety of the stupidity and wickedness of their victims. We may object to the fact that the only person in the play possessed of a scruple of honesty is discomfited, and that the greatest scoundrel of all is approved in the end and rewarded. The comedy is so admirably written and contrived, the personages stand out with such lifelike distinctness in their several kinds, and the whole is animated with such verve and resourcefulness that "The Alchemist" is a new marvel every time it is read. Lastly of this group comes the tremendous comedy, "Bartholomew Fair," less clear cut, less definite, and less structurally worthy of praise than its three predecessors, but full of the keenest and cleverest of satire and inventive to a degree beyond any English comedy save some other of Jonson's own. It is in "Bartholomew Fair" that we are presented to the immortal caricature of the Puritan, Zeal-in-the-Land Busy, and the Littlewits that group about him, and it is in this extraordinary comedy that the humour of Jonson, always open to this danger, loosens into the Rabelaisian mode that so delighted King James in "The Gipsies Metamorphosed." Another comedy of less merit is "The Devil is an Ass," acted in 1616. It was the failure of this play that caused Jonson to give over writing for the public stage for a period of nearly ten years.

"Volpone" was laid as to scene in Venice. Whether because of the success of "Eastward Hoe" or for other reasons, the other three comedies declare in the words of the prologue to "The Alchemist":

"Our scene is London, 'cause we would make known No country's mirth is better than our own."

Indeed Jonson went further when he came to revise his plays for collected publication in his folio of 1616, he transferred the scene of "Every Man in His Humour" from Florence to London also, converting Signior Lorenzo di Pazzi to Old Kno'well, Prospero to Master Welborn, and Hesperida to Dame Kitely "dwelling i' the Old Jewry."

In his comedies of London life, despite his trend towards caricature, Jonson has shown himself a genuine realist, drawing from the life about him with an experience and insight rare in any generation. A happy comparison has been suggested between Ben Jonson and Charles Dickens. Both were men of the people, lowly born and hardly bred. Each knew the London of his time as few men knew it; and each represented it intimately and in elaborate detail. Both men were at heart moralists, seeking the truth by the exaggerated methods of humour and caricature; perverse, even wrong-headed at times, but possessed of a true pathos and largeness of heart, and when all has been said — though the Elizabethan ran to satire, the Victorian to sentimentality — leaving the world better for the art that they practised in it.

In 1616, the year of the death of Shakespeare, Jonson collected his plays, his poetry, and his masques for publication in a collective edition. This was an unusual thing at the time and had been attempted by no dramatist before Jonson. This volume published, in a carefully revised text, all the plays thus far mentioned, excepting "The Case is Altered," which Jonson did not acknowledge, "Bartholomew Fair," and "The Devil is an Ass," which was written too late. It included likewise a book of some hundred and thirty odd "Epigrams," in which form of brief and pungent writing Jonson was an acknowledged master; "The Forest," a smaller collection of lyric and occasional verse and some ten "Masques" and "Entertainments." In this same year Jonson was made poet laureate with a pension of one hundred marks a year. This, with his fees and returns from several noblemen, and the small earnings of his plays must have formed the bulk of his income. The poet appears to have done certain literary hack-work for others, as, for example, parts of the Punic Wars contributed to Raleigh's "History of the World." We know from a story, little to the credit of either, that Jonson accompanied Raleigh's son abroad in the capacity of a tutor. In 1618 Jonson was granted the reversion of the office of Master of the Revels, a post for which he was peculiarly fitted; but he did not live to enjoy its perquisites. Jonson was honoured with degrees by both universities, though when and under what circumstances is not known. It has been said that he narrowly escaped the honour of knighthood, which the satirists of the day averred King James was wont to lavish with an indiscriminate hand. Worse men were made knights in his day than worthy Ben Jonson.

From 1616 to the close of the reign of King James, Jonson produced nothing for the stage. But he "prosecuted" what he calls "his wonted studies" with such assiduity that he became in reality, as by report, one of the most learned men of his time. Jonson's theory of authorship involved a wide acquaintance with books and "an ability," as he put it, "to convert the substance or riches of another poet to his own use." Accordingly Jonson read not only the Greek and Latin classics down to the lesser writers, but he acquainted himself especially with the Latin writings of his learned contemporaries, their prose as well as their poetry, their antiquities and curious lore as well as their more solid learning. Though a poor man, Jonson was an indefatigable collector of books. He told Drummond that "the Earl of Pembroke sent him 20 pounds every first day of the new year to buy new books." Unhappily, in 1623, his library was destroyed by fire, an accident serio-comically described in his witty poem, "An Execration upon Vulcan." Yet even now a book turns up from time to time in which is inscribed, in fair large Italian lettering, the name, Ben Jonson. With respect to Jonson's use of his material, Dryden said memorably of him: "[He] was not only a professed imitator of Horace, but a learned plagiary of all the others; you track him everywhere in their snow....But he has done his robberies so openly that one sees he fears not to be taxed by any law. He invades authors like a monarch, and what would be theft in other poets is only victory in him." And yet it is but fair to say that Jonson prided himself, and justly, on his originality. In "Catiline," he not only uses Sallust's account of the conspiracy, but he models some of the speeches of Cicero on the Roman orator's actual words. In "Poetaster," he lifts a whole satire out of Horace and dramatises it effectively for his purposes. The sophist Libanius suggests the situation of "The Silent Woman"; a Latin comedy of Giordano Bruno, "Il Candelaio," the relation of the dupes and the sharpers in "The Alchemist," the "Mostellaria" of Plautus, its admirable opening scene. But Jonson commonly bettered his sources, and putting the stamp of his sovereignty on whatever bullion he borrowed made it thenceforward to all time current and his own.

The lyric and especially the occasional poetry of Jonson has a peculiar merit. His theory demanded design and the perfection of literary finish. He was furthest from the rhapsodist and the careless singer of an idle day; and he believed that Apollo could only be worthily served in singing robes and laurel crowned. And yet many of Jonson's lyrics will live as long as the language. Who does not know "Queen and huntress, chaste and fair." "Drink to me only with thine eyes," or "Still to be neat, still to be dressed"? Beautiful in form, deft and graceful in expression, with not a word too much or one that bears not its part in the total effect, there is yet about the lyrics of Jonson a certain stiffness and formality, a suspicion that they were not quite spontaneous and unbidden, but that they were carved, so to speak, with disproportionate labour by a potent man of letters whose habitual thought is on greater things. It is for these reasons that Jonson is even better in the epigram and in occasional verse where rhetorical finish and pointed wit less interfere with the spontaneity and emotion which we usually associate with lyrical poetry. There are no such epitaphs as Ben Jonson's, witness the charming ones on his own children, on Salathiel Pavy, the child-actor, and many more; and this even though the rigid law of mine and thine must now restore to William Browne of Tavistock the famous lines beginning: "Underneath this sable hearse." Jonson is unsurpassed, too, in the difficult poetry of compliment, seldom falling into fulsome praise and disproportionate similitude, yet showing again and again a generous appreciation of worth in others, a discriminating taste and a generous personal regard. There was no man in England of his rank so well known and universally beloved as Ben Jonson. The list of his friends, of those to whom he had written verses, and those who had written verses to him, includes the name of every man of prominence in the England of King James. And the tone of many of these productions discloses an affectionate familiarity that speaks for the amiable personality and sound worth of the laureate. In 1619, growing unwieldy through inactivity, Jonson hit upon the heroic remedy of a journey afoot to Scotland. On his way thither and back he was hospitably received at the houses of many friends and by those to whom his friends had recommended him. When he arrived in Edinburgh, the burgesses met to grant him the freedom of the city, and Drummond, foremost of Scottish poets, was proud to entertain him for weeks as his guest at Hawthornden. Some of the noblest of Jonson's poems were inspired by friendship. Such is the fine "Ode to the memory of Sir Lucius Cary and Sir Henry Moryson," and that admirable piece of critical insight and filial affection, prefixed to the first Shakespeare folio, "To the memory of my beloved master, William Shakespeare, and what he hath left us," to mention only these. Nor can the earlier "Epode," beginning "Not to know vice at all," be matched in stately gravity and gnomic wisdom in its own wise and stately age.

But if Jonson had deserted the stage after the publication of his folio and up to the end of the reign of King James, he was far from inactive; for year after year his inexhaustible inventiveness continued to contribute to the masquing and entertainment at court. In "The Golden Age Restored," Pallas turns the Iron Age with its attendant evils into statues which sink out of sight; in "Pleasure Reconciled to Virtue," Atlas figures represented as an old man, his shoulders covered with snow, and Comus, "the god of cheer or the belly," is one of the characters, a circumstance which an imaginative boy of ten, named John Milton, was not to forget. "Pan's Anniversary," late in the reign of James, proclaimed that Jonson had not yet forgotten how to write exquisite lyrics, and "The Gipsies Metamorphosed" displayed the old drollery and broad humorous stroke still unimpaired and unmatchable. These, too, and the earlier years of Charles were the days of the Apollo Room of the Devil

Tavern where Jonson presided, the absolute monarch of English literary Bohemia. We hear of a room blazoned about with Jonson's own judicious "Leges Convivales" in letters of gold, of a company made up of the choicest spirits of the time, devotedly attached to their veteran dictator, his reminiscences, opinions, affections, and enmities. And we hear, too, of valorous potations; but in the words of Herrick addressed to his master, Jonson, at the Devil Tavern, as at the Dog, the Triple Tun, and at the Mermaid,

> *"We such clusters had*
> *As made us nobly wild, not mad,*
> *And yet each verse of thine*
> *Outdid the meat, outdid the frolic wine."*

But the patronage of the court failed in the days of King Charles, though Jonson was not without royal favours; and the old poet returned to the stage, producing, between 1625 and 1633, "The Staple of News," "The New Inn," "The Magnetic Lady," and "The Tale of a Tub," the last doubtless revised from a much earlier comedy. None of these plays met with any marked success, although the scathing generalisation of Dryden that designated them "Jonson's dotages" is unfair to their genuine merits. Thus the idea of an office for the gathering, proper dressing, and promulgation of news (wild flight of the fancy in its time) was an excellent subject for satire on the existing absurdities among newsmongers; although as much can hardly be said for "The Magnetic Lady," who, in her bounty, draws to her personages of differing humours to reconcile them in the end according to the alternative title, or "Humours Reconciled." These last plays of the old dramatist revert to caricature and the hard lines of allegory; the moralist is more than ever present, the satire degenerates into personal lampoon, especially of his sometime friend, Inigo Jones, who appears unworthily to have used his influence at court against the broken-down old poet. And now disease claimed Jonson, and he was bedridden for months. He had succeeded Middleton in 1628 as Chronologer to the City of London, but lost the post for not fulfilling its duties. King Charles befriended him, and even commissioned him to write still for the entertainment of the court; and he was not without the sustaining hand of noble patrons and devoted friends among the younger poets who were proud to be "sealed of the tribe of Ben."

Jonson died, August 6, 1637, and a second folio of his works, which he had been some time gathering, was printed in 1640, bearing in its various parts dates ranging from 1630 to 1642. It included all the plays mentioned in the foregoing paragraphs, excepting "The Case is Altered;" the masques, some fifteen, that date between 1617 and 1630; another collection of lyrics and occasional poetry called "Underwoods", including some further entertainments; a translation of "Horace's Art of Poetry" (also published in a vicesimo quarto in 1640), and certain fragments and ingatherings which the poet would hardly have included himself. These last comprise the fragment (less than seventy lines) of a tragedy called "Mortimer his Fall," and three acts of a pastoral drama of much beauty and poetic spirit, "The Sad Shepherd." There is also the exceedingly interesting "English Grammar" "made by Ben Jonson for the benefit of all strangers out of his observation of the English language now spoken and in use," in Latin and English; and "Timber, or Discoveries" "made upon men and matter as they have flowed out of his daily reading, or had their reflux to his peculiar notion of the times." The "Discoveries," as it is usually called, is a commonplace book such as many literary men have kept, in which their reading was chronicled, passages that took their fancy translated or transcribed, and their passing opinions noted. Many passages of Jonson's "Discoveries" are literal translations from the authors he chanced to be reading, with the reference, noted or not, as the accident of the moment prescribed. At times he follows the line of Macchiavelli's argument as to the nature and conduct of princes; at others he clarifies his own conception of poetry and poets by recourse to Aristotle. He finds a choice paragraph on eloquence in Seneca the elder and applies it to his own recollection of Bacon's power as an orator; and another on facile and ready genius, and translates it, adapting it to his recollection of his fellow-playwright, Shakespeare. To call such passages — which Jonson never intended for publication — plagiarism, is to obscure the significance of words. To disparage his memory by citing them is a preposterous use of scholarship. Jonson's prose, both in his dramas, in the descriptive comments of his masques, and in the "Discoveries," is characterised by clarity and vigorous directness, nor is it wanting in a fine sense of form or in the subtler graces of diction.

When Jonson died there was a project for a handsome monument to his memory. But the Civil War was at hand, and the project failed. A memorial, not insufficient, was carved on the stone covering his grave in one of the aisles of Westminster Abbey:

"O rare Ben Jonson."

FELIX E. SCHELLING
THE COLLEGE, PHILADELPHIA, U.S.A.

EPICOENE; OR, THE SILENT WOMAN

TO THE TRULY NOBLE BY ALL TITLES SIR FRANCIS STUART

Sir,

My hope is not so nourished by example, as it will conclude, this dumb piece should please you, because it hath pleased others before; but by trust, that when you have read it, you will find it worthy to have displeased none. This makes that I now number you, not only in the names of favour, but the names of justice to what I write; and do presently call you to the exercise of that noblest, and manliest virtue; as coveting rather to be freed in my fame, by the authority of a judge, than the credit of an undertaker. Read, therefore, I pray you, and censure. There is not a line, or syllable in it, changed from the simplicity of the first copy. And, when you shall consider, through the certain hatred of some, how much a man's innocency may be endangered by an uncertain accusation; you will, I doubt not, so begin to hate the iniquity of such natures, as I shall love the contumely done me, whose end was so honourable as to be wiped off by your sentence.

Your unprofitable, but true Lover,

BEN JONSON

DRAMATIS PERSONAE

MOROSE, a Gentleman that loves no noise.
SIR DAUPHINE EUGENIE, a Knight, his Nephew.
NED CLERIMONT, a Gentleman, his Friend.
TRUEWIT, another Friend.
SIR JOHN DAW, a Knight.
SIR AMOROUS LA-FOOLE, a Knight also.
THOMAS OTTER, a Land and Sea Captain.
CUTBEARD, a Barber.
MUTE, one of MOROSE's Servants.
PARSON
Page to CLERIMONT.
EPICOENE, supposed the Silent Woman.
LADY HAUGHTY, LADY CENTAURE, MISTRESS DOL MAVIS, Ladies Collegiates.
MISTRESS OTTER, the Captain's Wife, MISTRESS TRUSTY, LADY HAUGHTY'S Woman, Pretenders.
Pages, Servants, etc.
SCENE — LONDON.

2

PROLOGUE

Truth says, of old the art of making plays
Was to content the people; and their praise
Was to the poet money, wine, and bays.

But in this age, a sect of writers are,
That, only, for particular likings care,
And will taste nothing that is popular.

With such we mingle neither brains nor breasts;
Our wishes, like to those make public feasts,
Are not to please the cook's taste, but the guests'.

Yet, if those cunning palates hither come,
They shall find guests' entreaty, and good room;
And though all relish not, sure there will be some,

That, when they leave their seats, shall make them say,
Who wrote that piece, could so have wrote a play,
But that he knew this was the better way.

For, to present all custard, or all tart,
And have no other meats, to bear a part.
Or to want bread, and salt, were but course art.

The poet prays you then, with better thought
To sit; and, when his cates are all in brought,
Though there be none far-fet, there will dear-bought,

Be fit for ladies: some for lords, knights, 'squires;
Some for your waiting-wench, and city-wires;
Some for your men, and daughters of Whitefriars.

Nor is it, only, while you keep your seat
Here, that his feast will last; but you shall eat
A week at ord'naries, on his broken meat:
  If his muse be true,
  Who commends her to you.

ANOTHER

The ends of all, who for the scene do write,
Are, or should be, to profit and delight.
And still't hath been the praise of all best times,
So persons were not touch'd, to tax the crimes.
Then, in this play, which we present to-night,
And make the object of your ear and sight,
On forfeit of yourselves, think nothing true:
Lest so you make the maker to judge you,
For he knows, poet never credit gain'd
By writing truths, but things (like truths) well feign'd.
If any yet will, with particular sleight
Of application, wrest what he doth write;
And that he meant, or him, or her, will say:
They make a libel, which he made a play.

ACT 1

SCENE 1.1.

A ROOM IN CLERIMONT'S HOUSE.

ENTER CLERIMONT, MAKING HIMSELF READY, FOLLOWED BY HIS PAGE.

CLER: Have you got the song yet perfect, I gave you, boy?

PAGE: Yes, sir.

CLER: Let me hear it.

PAGE: You shall, sir, but i'faith let nobody else.

CLER: Why, I pray?

PAGE: It will get you the dangerous name of a poet in town, sir; besides me a perfect deal of ill-will at the mansion you wot of, whose lady is the argument of it; where now I am the welcomest thing under a man that comes there.

CLER: I think, and above a man too, if the truth were rack'd out of you.

PAGE: No, faith, I'll confess before, sir. The gentlewomen play with me, and throw me on the bed; and carry me in to my lady; and she kisses me with her oil'd face; and puts a peruke on my head; and asks me an I will wear her gown? and I say, no: and then she hits me a blow o' the ear, and calls me Innocent! and lets me go.

CLER: No marvel if the door be kept shut against your master, when the entrance is so easy to you—well sir, you shall go there no more, lest I be fain to seek your voice in my lady's rushes, a fortnight hence. Sing, sir.

PAGE [SINGS]: Still to be neat, still to be drest—

5

[ENTER TRUEWIT.]

TRUE: Why, here's the man that can melt away his time and never feels it! What between his mistress abroad, and his ingle at home, high fare, soft lodging, fine clothes, and his fiddle; he thinks the hours have no wings, or the day no post-horse. Well, sir gallant, were you struck with the plague this minute, or condemn'd to any capital punishment to-morrow, you would begin then to think, and value every article of your time, esteem it at the true rate, and give all for it.

CLER: Why what should a man do?

TRUE: Why, nothing; or that which, when it is done, is as idle. Harken after the next horse-race or hunting-match; lay wagers, praise Puppy, or Pepper-corn, White-foot, Franklin; swear upon Whitemane's party; speak aloud, that my lords may hear you; visit my ladies at night, and be able to give them the character of every bowler or better on the green. These be the things wherein your fashionable men exercise themselves, and I for company.

CLER: Nay, if I have thy authority, I'll not leave yet. Come, the other are considerations, when we come to have gray heads and weak hams, moist eyes and shrunk members. We'll think on 'em then; and we'll pray and fast.

TRUE: Ay, and destine only that time of age to goodness, which our want of ability will not let us employ in evil!

CLER: Why, then 'tis time enough.

TRUE: Yes; as if a man should sleep all the term, and think to effect his business the last day. O, Clerimont, this time, because it is an incorporeal thing, and not subject to sense, we mock ourselves the fineliest out of it, with vanity and misery indeed! not seeking an end of wretchedness, but only changing the matter still.

CLER: Nay, thou wilt not leave now—

TRUE: See but our common disease! with what justice can we complain, that great men will not look upon us, nor be at leisure to

6

give our affairs such dispatch as we expect, when we will never do it to ourselves? nor hear, nor regard ourselves?

CLER: Foh! thou hast read Plutarch's morals, now, or some such tedious fellow; and it shews so vilely with thee! 'fore God, 'twill spoil thy wit utterly. Talk me of pins, and feathers, and ladies, and rushes, and such things: and leave this Stoicity alone, till thou mak'st sermons.

TRUE: Well, sir; if it will not take, I have learn'd to lose as little of my kindness as I can. I'll do good to no man against his will, certainly. When were you at the college?

CLER: What college?

TRUE: As if you knew not!

CLER: No faith, I came but from court yesterday.

TRUE: Why, is it not arrived there yet, the news? A new foundation, sir, here in the town, of ladies, that call themselves the collegiates, an order between courtiers and country-madams that live from their husbands; and give entertainment to all the wits, and braveries of the time, as they call them: cry down, or up, what they like or dislike in a brain or a fashion, with most masculine, or rather hermaphroditical authority; and every day gain to their college some new probationer.

CLER: Who is the president?

TRUE: The grave, and youthful matron, the lady Haughty.

CLER: A pox of her autumnal face, her pieced beauty! there's no man can be admitted till she be ready, now-a-days, till she has painted, and perfumed, and wash'd, and scour'd, but the boy here; and him she wipes her oil'd lips upon, like a sponge. I have made a song, I pray thee hear it, on the subject.

PAGE. [SINGS.]

Still to be neat, still to be drest,
As you were going to a feast;
Still to be powder'd, still perfum'd;
Lady, it is to be presumed,

7

Though art's hid causes are not found,
All is not sweet, all is not sound.

Give me a look, give me a face,
That makes simplicity a grace;
Robes loosely flowing, hair as free:
Such sweet neglect more taketh me,
Then all the adulteries of art;
They strike mine eyes, but not my heart.

TRUE: And I am clearly on the other side: I love a good dressing
before any beauty o' the world. O, a woman is then like a
delicate garden; nor is there one kind of it; she may vary every
hour; take often counsel of her glass, and choose the best. If
she have good ears, shew them; good hair, lay it out; good
legs, wear short clothes; a good hand, discover it often;
practise any art to mend breath, cleanse teeth, repair eye-brows;
paint, and profess it.

CLER: How? publicly?

TRUE: The doing of it, not the manner: that must be private.
Many things that seem foul in the doing, do please done. A lady
should, indeed, study her face, when we think she sleeps; nor,
when the doors are shut, should men be enquiring; all is sacred
within, then. Is it for us to see their perukes put on, their
false teeth, their complexion, their eye-brows, their nails? You
see guilders will not work, but inclosed. They must not discover
how little serves, with the help of art, to adorn a great deal.
How long did the canvas hang afore Aldgate? Were the people
suffered to see the city's Love and Charity, while they were rude
stone, before they were painted and burnish'd? No: no more
should Servants approach their mistresses, but when they are
complete and finish'd.

CLER: Well said, my Truewit.

TRUE: And a wise lady will keep a guard always upon the place,
that she may do things securely. I once followed a rude fellow into
a chamber, where the poor madam, for haste, and troubled,
snatch'd at her peruke to cover her baldness; and put it on the
wrong way.

CLER: O prodigy!

8

TRUE: And the unconscionable knave held her in complement an hour with that reverst face, when I still look'd when she should talk from the t'other side.

CLER: Why, thou shouldst have relieved her.

TRUE: No, faith, I let her alone, as we'll let this argument, if you please, and pass to another. When saw you Dauphine Eugenie?

CLER: Not these three days. Shall we go to him this morning? he is very melancholy, I hear.

TRUE: Sick of the uncle? is he? I met that stiff piece of formality, his uncle, yesterday, with a huge turban of night-caps on his head, buckled over his ears.

CLER: O, that's his custom when he walks abroad. He can endure no noise, man.

TRUE: So I have heard. But is the disease so ridiculous in him as it is made? They say he has been upon divers treaties with the fish-wives and orange-women; and articles propounded between them: marry, the chimney-sweepers will not be drawn in.

CLER: No, nor the broom-men: they stand out stiffly. He cannot endure a costard-monger, he swoons if he hear one.

TRUE: Methinks a smith should be ominous.

CLER: Or any hammer-man. A brasier is not suffer'd to dwell in the parish, nor an armourer. He would have hang'd a pewterer's prentice once on a Shrove-tuesday's riot, for being of that trade, when the rest were quit.

TRUE: A trumpet should fright him terribly, or the hautboys.

CLER: Out of his senses. The waights of the city have a pension of him not to come near that ward. This youth practised on him one night like the bell-man; and never left till he had brought him down to the door with a long-sword: and there left him flourishing with the air.

PAGE: Why, sir, he hath chosen a street to lie in so narrow at both ends, that it will receive no coaches, nor carts, nor any of these

9

common noises: and therefore we that love him, devise to bring him in such as we may, now and then, for his exercise, to breathe him. He would grow resty else in his ease: his virtue would rust without action. I entreated a bearward, one day, to come down with the dogs of some four parishes that way, and I thank him he did; and cried his games under master Morose's window: till he was sent crying away, with his head made a most bleeding spectacle to the multitude. And, another time, a fencer marchng to his prize, had his drum most tragically run through, for taking that street in his way at my request.

TRUE: A good wag! How does he for the bells?

CLER: O, in the Queen's time, he was wont to go out of town every Saturday at ten o'clock, or on holy day eves. But now, by reason of the sickness, the perpetuity of ringing has made him devise a room, with double walls, and treble ceilings; the windows close shut and caulk'd: and there he lives by candlelight. He turn'd away a man, last week, for having a pair of new shoes that creak'd. And this fellow waits on him now in tennis-court socks, or slippers soled with wool: and they talk each to other in a trunk. See, who comes here!

[ENTER SIR DAUPHINE EUGENIE.]

DAUP: How now! what ail you sirs? dumb?

TRUE: Struck into stone, almost, I am here, with tales o' thine uncle. There was never such a prodigy heard of.

DAUP: I would you would once lose this subject, my masters, for my sake. They are such as you are, that have brought me into that predicament I am with him.

TRUE: How is that?

DAUP: Marry, that he will disinherit me; no more. He thinks, I and my company are authors of all the ridiculous Acts and Monuments are told of him.

TRUE: S'lid, I would be the author of more to vex him; that purpose deserves it: it gives thee law of plaguing him. I will tell thee what I would do. I would make a false almanack; get it printed: and then have him drawn out on a coronation day to the

Tower-wharf, and kill him with the noise of the ordnance. Disinherit thee! he cannot, man. Art not thou next of blood, and his sister's son?

DAUP: Ay, but he will thrust me out of it, he vows, and marry.

TRUE: How! that's a more portent. Can he endure no noise, and will venture on a wife?

CLER: Yes: why thou art a stranger, it seems, to his best trick, yet. He has employed a fellow this half year all over England to hearken him out a dumb woman; be she of any form, or any quality, so she be able to bear children: her silence is dowry enough, he says.

TRUE: But I trust to God he has found none.

CLER: No; but he has heard of one that is lodged in the next street to him, who is exceedingly soft-spoken; thrifty of her speech; that spends but six words a day. And her he's about now, and shall have her.

TRUE: Is't possible! who is his agent in the business?

CLER: Marry a barber; one Cutbeard; an honest fellow, one that tells Dauphine all here.

TRUE: Why you oppress me with wonder: a woman, and a barber, and love no noise!

CLER: Yes, faith. The fellow trims him silently, and has not the knack with his sheers or his fingers: and that continence in a barber he thinks so eminent a virtue, as it has made him chief of his counsel.

TRUE: Is the barber to be seen, or the wench?

CLER: Yes, that they are.

TRUE: I prithee, Dauphine, let us go thither.

DAUP: I have some business now: I cannot, i'faith.

TRUE: You shall have no business shall make you neglect this, sir;

11

we'll make her talk, believe it; or, if she will not, we can give out at least so much as shall interrupt the treaty; we will break it. Thou art bound in conscience, when he suspects thee without cause, to torment him.

DAUP: Not I, by any means. I will give no suffrage to't. He shall never have that plea against me, that I opposed the least phant'sy of his. Let it lie upon my stars to be guilty, I'll be innocent.

TRUE: Yes, and be poor, and beg; do, innocent: when some groom of his has got him an heir, or this barber, if he himself cannot. Innocent!—I prithee, Ned, where lies she? let him be innocent still.

CLER: Why, right over against the barber's; in the house where sir John Daw lies.

TRUE: You do not mean to confound me!

CLER: Why?

TRUE: Does he that would marry her know so much?

CLER: I cannot tell.

TRUE: 'Twere enough of imputation to her with him.

CLER: Why?

TRUE: The only talking sir in the town! Jack Daw! and he teach her not to speak!—God be wi' you. I have some business too.

CLER: Will you not go thither, then?

TRUE: Not with the danger to meet Daw, for mine ears.

CLER: Why? I thought you two had been upon very good terms.

TRUE: Yes, of keeping distance.

CLER: They say, he is a very good scholar.

TRUE: Ay, and he says it first. A pox on him, a fellow that

pretends only to learning, buys titles, and nothing else of books in him!

CLER: The world reports him to be very learned.

TRUE: I am sorry the world should so conspire to belie him.

CLER: Good faith, I have heard very good things come from him.

TRUE: You may; there's none so desperately ignorant to deny that: would they were his own! God be wi' you, gentleman.

[EXIT HASTILY.]

CLER: This is very abrupt!

DAUP: Come, you are a strange open man, to tell every thing thus.

CLER: Why, believe it, Dauphine, Truewit's a very honest fellow.

DAUP: I think no other: but this frank nature of his is not for secrets.

CLER: Nay, then, you are mistaken, Dauphine: I know where he has been well trusted, and discharged the trust very truly, and heartily.

DAUP: I contend not, Ned; but with the fewer a business is carried, it is ever the safer. Now we are alone, if you will go thither, I am for you.

CLER: When were you there?

DAUP: Last night: and such a Decameron of sport fallen out! Boccace never thought of the like. Daw does nothing but court her; and the wrong way. He would lie with her, and praises her modesty; desires that she would talk and be free, and commends her silence in verses: which he reads, and swears are the best that ever man made. Then rails at his fortunes, stamps, and mutines, why he is not made a counsellor, and call'd to affairs of state.

CLER: I prithee let's go. I would fain partake this. Some water, boy.

[EXIT PAGE.]

DAUP: We are invited to dinner together, he and I, by one that came thither to him, sir La-Foole.

CLER: O, that's a precious mannikin.

DAUP: Do you know him?

CLER: Ay, and he will know you too, if e'er he saw you but once, though you should meet him at church in the midst of prayers. He is one of the braveries, though he be none of the wits. He will salute a judge upon the bench, and a bishop in the pulpit, a lawyer when he is pleading at the bar, and a lady when she is dancing in a masque, and put her out. He does give plays, and suppers, and invites his guests to them, aloud, out of his window, as they ride by in coaches. He has a lodging in the Strand for the purpose: or to watch when ladies are gone to the china-houses, or the Exchange, that he may meet them by chance, and give them presents, some two or three hundred pounds' worth of toys, to be laugh'd at. He is never without a spare banquet, or sweet-meats in his chamber, for their women to alight at, and come up to for a bait.

DAUP: Excellent! he was a fine youth last night; but now he is much finer! what is his Christian name? I have forgot.

[RE-ENTER PAGE.]

CLER: Sir Amorous La-Foole.

PAGE: The gentleman is here below that owns that name.

CLER: 'Heart, he's come to invite me to dinner, I hold my life.

DAUP: Like enough: prithee, let's have him up.

CLER: Boy, marshal him.

PAGE: With a truncheon, sir?

CLER: Away, I beseech you.
[EXIT PAGE.]
I'll make him tell us his pedigree, now; and what meat he has to

14

dinner; and who are his guests; and the whole course of his fortunes: with a breath.

[ENTER SIR AMOROUS LA-FOOLE.]

LA-F: 'Save, dear sir Dauphine! honoured master Clerimont!

CLER: Sir Amorous! you have very much honested my lodging with your presence.

LA-F: Good faith, it is a fine lodging: almost as delicate a lodging as mine.

CLER: Not so, sir.

LA-F: Excuse me, sir, if it were in the Strand, I assure you. I am come, master Clerimont, to entreat you to wait upon two or three ladies, to dinner, to-day.

CLER: How, sir! wait upon them? did you ever see me carry dishes?

LA-F: No, sir, dispense with me; I meant, to bear them company.

CLER: O, that I will, sir: the doubtfulness of your phrase, believe it, sir, would breed you a quarrel once an hour, with the terrible boys, if you should but keep them fellowship a day.

LA-F: It should be extremely against my will, sir, if I contested with any man.

CLER: I believe it, sir; where hold you your feast?

LA-F: At Tom Otter's, sir.

PAGE: Tom Otter? what's he?

LA-F: Captain Otter, sir; he is a kind of gamester, but he has had command both by sea and by land.

PAGE: O, then he is animal amphibium?

LA-F: Ay, sir: his wife was the rich china-woman, that the

15

courtiers visited so often; that gave the rare entertainment. She commands all at home.

CLER: Then she is captain Otter.

LA-F: You say very well, sir: she is my kinswoman, a La-Foole by the mother-side, and will invite any great ladies for my sake.

PAGE: Not of the La-Fooles of Essex?

LA-F: No, sir, the La-Fooles of London.

CLER: Now, he's in. [ASIDE.]

LA-F: They all come out of our house, the La-Fooles of the north, the La-Fooles of the west, the La-Fooles of the east and south—we are as ancient a family as any is in Europe—but I myself am descended lineally of the French La-Fooles—and, we do bear for our coat yellow, or or, checker'd azure, and gules, and some three or four colours more, which is a very noted coat, and has, sometimes, been solemnly worn by divers nobility of our house but let that go, antiquity is not respected now.—I had a brace of fat does sent me, gentlemen, and half a dozen of pheasants, a dozen or two of godwits, and some other fowl, which I would have eaten, while they are good, and in good company:—there will be a great lady, or two, my lady Haughty, my lady Centaure, mistress Dol Mavis—and they come o' purpose to see the silent gentlewoman, mistress Epicoene, that honest sir John Daw has promis'd to bring thither—and then, mistress Trusty, my lady's woman, will be there too, and this honourable knight, sir Dauphine, with yourself, master Clerimont—and we'll be very merry, and have fidlers, and dance.—I have been a mad wag in my time, and have spent some crowns since I was a page in court, to my lord Lofty, and after, my lady's gentleman-usher, who got me knighted in Ireland, since it pleased my elder brother to die.—I had as fair a gold jerkin on that day, as any worn in the island voyage, or at Cadiz, none dispraised; and I came over in it hither, shew'd myself to my friends in court, and after went down to my tenants in the country, and surveyed my lands, let new leases, took their money, spent it in the eye o' the land here, upon ladies:—and now I can take up at my pleasure.

DAUP: Can you take up ladies, sir?

16

CLER: O, let him breathe, he has not recover'd.

DAUP: Would I were your half in that commodity!

LA-F.: No, sir, excuse me: I meant money, which can take up any thing. I have another guest or two, to invite, and say as much to, gentlemen. I will take my leave abruptly, in hope you will not fail—Your servant.

[EXIT.]

DAUP: We will not fail you, sir precious La-Foole; but she shall, that your ladies come to see, if I have credit afore sir Daw.

CLER: Did you ever hear such a wind-sucker, as this?

DAUP: Or, such a rook as the other! that will betray his mistress to be seen! Come, 'tis time we prevented it.

CLER: Go.

[EXEUNT.]

ACT 2

SCENE 2.1.

A ROOM IN MOROSE'S HOUSE.

ENTER MOROSE, WITH A TUBE IN HIS HAND, FOLLOWED BY MUTE.

MOR: Cannot I, yet, find out a more compendious method, than by this trunk, to save my servants the labour of speech, and mine ears the discord of sounds? Let me see: all discourses but my own afflict me, they seem harsh, impertinent, and irksome. Is it not possible, that thou should'st answer me by signs, and I apprehend thee, fellow? Speak not, though I question you. You have taken the ring off from the street door, as I bade you? answer me not by speech, but by silence; unless it be otherwise
[MUTE MAKES A LEG.]
—very good. And you have fastened on a thick quilt, or flock-bed, on the outside of the door; that if they knock with their daggers, or with brick-bats, they can make no noise?—But with your leg, your answer, unless it be otherwise,
[MUTE MAKES A LEG.]
—Very good. This is not only fit modesty in a servant, but good state and discretion in a master. And you have been with Cutbeard the barber, to have him come to me?
[MUTE MAKES A LEG.]
—Good. And, he will come presently? Answer me not but with your leg, unless it be otherwise: if it be otherwise, shake your head, or shrug.
[MUTE MAKES A LEG.]
—So! Your Italian and Spaniard are wise in these: and it is a frugal and comely gravity. How long will it be ere Cutbeard come? Stay, if an hour, hold up your whole hand, if half an hour, two fingers; if a quarter, one;
[MUTE HOLDS UP A FINGER BENT.]
—Good: half a quarter? 'tis well. And have you given him a key, to come in without knocking?
[MUTE MAKES A LEG.]
—good. And is the lock oil'd, and the hinges, to-day?
[MUTE MAKES A LEG.]

18

—good. And the quilting of the stairs no where worn out, and bare?

[MUTE MAKES A LEG.]

—Very good. I see, by much doctrine, and impulsion, it may be effected: stand by. The Turk, in this divine discipline, is admirable, exceeding all the potentates of the earth; still waited on by mutes; and all his commands so executed; yea, even in the war, as I have heard, and in his marches, most of his charges and directions given by signs, and with silence: an exquisite art! and I am heartily ashamed, and angry oftentimes, that the princes of Christendom should suffer a barbarian to transcend them in so high a point of felicity. I will practise it hereafter.

[A HORN WINDED WITHIN.]

—How now? oh! oh! what villain, what prodigy of mankind is that? look.

[EXIT MUTE.]

—[HORN AGAIN.]

—Oh! cut his throat, cut his throat! what murderer, hell-hound, devil can this be?

[RE-ENTER MUTE.]

MUTE: It is a post from the court—

MOR: Out rogue! and must thou blow thy horn too?

MUTE: Alas, it is a post from the court, sir, that says, he must speak with you, pain of death—

MOR: Pain of thy life, be silent!

[ENTER TRUEWIT WITH A POST-HORN, AND A HALTER IN HIS HAND.]

TRUE: By your leave, sir;—I am a stranger here:—Is your name master Morose? is your name master Morose? Fishes! Pythagoreans all! This is strange. What say you, sir? nothing? Has Harpocrates been here with his club, among you? Well sir, I will believe you to be the man at this time: I will venture upon you, sir. Your friends at court commend them to you, sir—

MOR: O men! O manners! was there ever such an impudence?

TRUE: And are extremely solicitous for you, sir.

19

MOR: Whose knave are you?

TRUE: Mine own knave, and your compeer, sir.

MOR: Fetch me my sword—

TRUE: You shall taste the one half of my dagger, if you do, groom;
and you, the other, if you stir, sir: Be patient, I charge you,
in the king's name, and hear me without insurrection. They say,
you are to marry; to marry! do you mark, sir?

MOR: How then, rude companion!

TRUE: Marry, your friends do wonder, sir, the Thames being so
near, wherein you may drown, so handsomely; or London-bridge,
at a low fall, with a fine leap, to hurry you down the stream; or,
such a delicate steeple, in the town as Bow, to vault from; or, a
braver height, as Paul's; Or, if you affected to do it nearer home,
and a shorter way, an excellent garret-window into the street; or,
a beam in the said garret, with this halter
[HE SHEWS HIM A HALTER.]—
which they have sent, and desire, that you would sooner commit
your grave head to this knot, than to the wedlock noose; or, take a
little sublimate, and go out of the world like a rat; or a fly,
as one said, with a straw in your arse: any way, rather than to
follow this goblin Matrimony. Alas, sir, do you ever think to
find a chaste wife in these times? now? when there are so many
masques, plays, Puritan preachings, mad folks, and other strange
sights to be seen daily, private and public? If you had lived
in king Ethelred's time, sir, or Edward the Confessor, you might,
perhaps, have found one in some cold country hamlet, then, a dull
frosty wench, would have been contented with one man: now, they
will as soon be pleased with one leg, or one eye. I'll tell you,
sir, the monstrous hazards you shall run with a wife.

MOR: Good sir, have I ever cozen'd any friends of yours of their
land? bought their possessions? taken forfeit of their mortgage?
begg'd a reversion from them? bastarded their issue? What have I
done, that may deserve this?

TRUE: Nothing, sir, that I know, but your itch of marriage.

MOR: Why? if I had made an assassinate upon your father,
vitiated your mother, ravished your sisters—

20

TRUE: I would kill you, sir, I would kill you, if you had.

MOR: Why, you do more in this, sir: it were a vengeance centuple, for all facinorous acts that could be named, to do that you do.

TRUE: Alas, sir, I am but a messenger: I but tell you, what you must hear. It seems your friends are careful after your soul's health, sir, and would have you know the danger: (but you may do your pleasure for all them, I persuade not, sir.) If, after you are married, your wife do run away with a vaulter, or the Frenchman that walks upon ropes, or him that dances the jig, or a fencer for his skill at his weapon; why it is not their fault, they have discharged their consciences; when you know what may happen. Nay, suffer valiantly, sir, for I must tell you all the perils that you are obnoxious to. If she be fair, young and vegetous, no sweet-meats ever drew more flies; all the yellow doublets and great roses in the town will be there. If foul and crooked, she'll be with them, and buy those doublets and roses, sir. If rich, and that you marry her dowry, not her, she'll reign in your house as imperious as a widow. If noble, all her kindred will be your tyrants. If fruitful, as proud as May, and humorous as April; she must have her doctors, her midwives, her nurses, her longings every hour; though it be for the dearest morsel of man. If learned, there was never such a parrot; all your patrimony will be too little for the guests that must be invited to hear her speak Latin and Greek; and you must lie with her in those languages too, if you will please her. If precise, you must feast all the silenced brethren, once in three days; salute the sisters; entertain the whole family, or wood of them; and hear long-winded exercises, singings and catechisings, which you are not given to, and yet must give for: to please the zealous matron your wife, who for the holy cause, will cozen you, over and above. You begin to sweat, sir! but this is not half, i'faith: you may do your pleasure, notwithstanding, as I said before: I come not to persuade you.
[MUTE IS STEALING AWAY.]
—Upon my faith, master servingman, if you do stir, I will beat you.

MOR: O, what is my sin! what is my sin!

TRUE: Then, if you love your wife, or rather dote on her, sir: O, how she'll torture you! and take pleasure in your torments! you shall lie with her but when she lists; she will not hurt her beauty, her complexion; or it must be for that jewel, or that pearl, when she does: every half hour's pleasure must be bought anew: and with the same pain and charge you woo'd her at first. Then you must keep what servants she please; what company she will; that friend must not visit you without her license; and him she loves most, she will seem to hate eagerliest, to decline your jealousy; or, feign to be jealous of you first; and for that cause go live with her she-friend, or cousin at the college, that can instruct her in all the mysteries of writing letters, corrupting servants, taming spies; where she must have that rich gown for such a great day; a new one for the next; a richer for the third; be served in silver; have the chamber fill'd with a succession of grooms, footmen, ushers, and other messengers; besides embroiderers, jewellers, tire-women, sempsters, feathermen, perfumers; whilst she feels not how the land drops away; nor the acres melt; nor foresees the change, when the mercer has your woods for her velvets; never weighs what her pride costs, sir: so she may kiss a page, or a smooth chin, that has the despair of a beard; be a stateswoman, know all the news, what was done at Salisbury, what at the Bath, what at court, what in progress; or, so she may censure poets, and authors, and styles, and compare them, Daniel with Spenser, Jonson with the t'other youth, and so forth: or be thought cunning in controversies, or the very knots of divinity; and have often in her mouth the state of the question: and then skip to the mathematics, and demonstration: and answer in religion to one, in state to another, in bawdry to a third.

MOR: O, O!

TRUE: All this is very true, sir. And then her going in disguise to that conjurer, and this cunning woman: where the first question is, how soon you shall die? next, if her present servant love her? next, if she shall have a new servant? and how many? which of her family would make the best bawd, male, or female? what precedence she shall have by her next match? and sets down the answers, and believes them above the scriptures. Nay, perhaps she will study the art.

MOR: Gentle sir, have you done? have you had your pleasure of me? I'll think of these things.

TRUE: Yes sir: and then comes reeking home of vapour and sweat, with going a foot, and lies in a month of a new face, all oil and birdlime; and rises in asses' milk, and is cleansed with a new

22

fucus: God be wi' you, sir. One thing more, which I had almost forgot. This too, with whom you are to marry, may have made a conveyance of her virginity afore hand, as your wise widows do of their states, before they marry, in trust to some friend, sir: who can tell? Or if she have not done it yet, she may do, upon the wedding-day, or the night before, and antedate you cuckold. The like has been heard of in nature. 'Tis no devised, impossible thing, sir. God be wi' you: I'll be bold to leave this rope with you, sir, for a remembrance. Farewell, Mute!

[EXIT.]

MOR: Come, have me to my chamber: but first shut the door.
[TRUEWIT WINDS THE HORN WITHOUT.]
O, shut the door, shut the door! is he come again?

[ENTER CUTBEARD.]

CUT: 'tis I, sir, your barber.

MOR: O, Cutbeard, Cutbeard, Cutbeard! here has been a cut-throat with me: help me in to my bed, and give me physic with thy counsel.

[EXEUNT.]

SCENE 2.2.

A ROOM IN SIR JOHN DAW'S HOUSE.

ENTER DAW, CLERIMONT, DAUPHINE, AND EPICOENE.

DAW: Nay, an she will, let her refuse at her own charges: 'tis nothing to me, gentlemen: but she will not be invited to the like feasts or guests every day.

CLER: O, by no means, she may not refuse—to stay at home, if you

23

love your reputation: 'Slight, you are invited thither o' purpose
to be seen, and laughed at by the lady of the college, and her
shadows. This trumpeter hath proclaim'd you.
[ASIDE TO EPICOENE.]

DAUP: You shall not go; let him be laugh'd at in your stead, for
not bringing you: and put him to his extemporal faculty of fooling
and talking loud, to satisfy the company.
[ASIDE TO EPICOENE.]

CLER: He will suspect us, talk aloud.—'Pray, mistress Epicoene,
let us see your verses; we have sir John Daw's leave: do not
conceal your servant's merit, and your own glories.

EPI: They'll prove my servant's glories, if you have his leave so
soon.

DAUP: His vain-glories, lady!

DAW: Shew them, shew them, mistress, I dare own them.

EPI: Judge you, what glories.

DAW: Nay, I'll read them myself too: an author must recite his
own works. It is a madrigal of Modesty.
Modest, and fair, for fair and good are near
Neighbours, howe'er.—

DAUP: Very good.

CLER: Ay, is't not?

DAW: No noble virtue ever was alone,
But two in one.

DAUP: Excellent!

CLER: That again, I pray, sir John.

DAUP: It has something in't like rare wit and sense.

CLER: Peace.

DAW: No noble virtue ever was alone,

24

But two in one.
Then, when I praise sweet modesty, I praise
Bright beauty's rays:
And having praised both beauty and modesty,
I have praised thee.

DAUP: Admirable!

CLER: How it chimes, and cries tink in the close, divinely!

DAUP: Ay, 'tis Seneca.

CLER: No, I think 'tis Plutarch.

DAW: The dor on Plutarch, and Seneca! I hate it: they are mine own imaginations, by that light. I wonder those fellows have such credit with gentlemen.

CLER: They are very grave authors.

DAW: Grave asses! mere essayists: a few loose sentences, and that's all. A man would talk so, his whole age: I do utter as good things every hour, if they were collected and observed, as either of them.

DAUP: Indeed, sir John!

CLER: He must needs; living among the wits and braveries too.

DAUP: Ay, and being president of them, as he is.

DAW: There's Aristotle, a mere common-place fellow; Plato, a discourser; Thucydides and Livy, tedious and dry; Tacitus, an entire knot: sometimes worth the untying, very seldom.

CLER: What do you think of the poets, sir John?

DAW: Not worthy to be named for authors. Homer, an old tedious, prolix ass, talks of curriers, and chines of beef. Virgil of dunging of land, and bees. Horace, of I know not what.

CLER: I think so.
DAW: And so Pindarus, Lycophron, Anacreon, Catullus, Seneca

the tragedian, Lucan, Propertius, Tibullus, Martial, Juvenal, Ausonius, Statius, Politian, Valerius Flaccus, and the rest—

CLER: What a sack full of their names he has got!

DAUP: And how he pours them out! Politian with Valerius Flaccus!

CLER: Was not the character right of him?

DAUP: As could be made, i'faith.

DAW: And Persius, a crabbed coxcomb, not to be endured.

DAUP: Why, whom do you account for authors, sir John Daw?

DAW: Syntagma juris civilis; Corpus juris civilis; Corpus juris canonici; the king of Spain's bible—

DAUP: Is the king of Spain's bible an author?

CLER: Yes, and Syntagma.

DAUP: What was that Syntagma, sir?

DAW: A civil lawyer, a Spaniard.

DAUP: Sure, Corpus was a Dutchman.

CLER: Ay, both the Corpuses, I knew 'em: they were very corpulent authors.

DAW: And, then there's Vatablus, Pomponatius, Symancha: the other are not to be received, within the thought of a scholar.

DAUP: 'Fore God, you have a simple learned servant, lady,— in titles. [ASIDE.]

CLER: I wonder that he is not called to the helm, and made a counsellor!

DAUP: He is one extraordinary.

CLER: Nay, but in ordinary: to say truth, the state wants such.

DAUP: Why that will follow.

CLER: I muse a mistress can be so silent to the dotes of such a servant.

DAW: 'Tis her virtue, sir. I have written somewhat of her silence too.

DAUP: In verse, sir John?

CLER: What else?

DAUP: Why? how can you justify your own being of a poet, that so slight all the old poets?

DAW: Why? every man that writes in verse is not a poet; you have of the wits that write verses, and yet are no poets: they are poets that live by it, the poor fellows that live by it.

DAUP: Why, would not you live by your verses, sir John?

CLER: No, 'twere pity he should. A knight live by his verses? he did not make them to that end, I hope.

DAUP: And yet the noble Sidney lives by his, and the noble family not ashamed.

CLER: Ay, he profest himself; but sir John Daw has more caution: he'll not hinder his own rising in the state so much. Do you think he will? Your verses, good sir John, and no poems.

DAW: Silence in woman, is like speech in man,
Deny't who can.

DAUP: Not I, believe it: your reason, sir.

DAW: Nor, is't a tale,
That female vice should be a virtue male,
Or masculine vice a female virtue be:
You shall it see
Prov'd with increase;
I know to speak, and she to hold her peace.
Do you conceive me, gentlemen?

27

DAUP: No, faith; how mean you "with increase," sir John?

DAW: Why, with increase is, when I court her for the common cause of mankind; and she says nothing, but "consentire videtur": and in time is gravida.

DAUP: Then this is a ballad of procreation?

CLER: A madrigal of procreation; you mistake.

EPI: 'Pray give me my verses again, servant.

DAW: If you'll ask them aloud, you shall.
[WALKS ASIDE WITH THE PAPERS.]

[ENTER TRUEWIT WITH HIS HORN.]

CLER: See, here's Truewit again!—Where hast thou been, in the name of madness! thus accoutred with thy horn?

TRUE: Where the sound of it might have pierced your sense with gladness, had you been in ear-reach of it. Dauphine, fall down and worship me: I have forbid the bans, lad: I have been with thy virtuous uncle, and have broke the match.

DAUP: You have not, I hope.

TRUE: Yes faith; if thou shouldst hope otherwise, I should repent me: this horn got me entrance; kiss it. I had no other way to get in, but by faining to be a post; but when I got in once, I proved none, but rather the contrary, turn'd him into a post, or a stone, or what is stiffer, with thundering into him the incommodities of a wife, and the miseries of marriage. If ever Gorgon were seen in the shape of a woman, he hath seen her in my description: I have put him off o' that scent for ever.—Why do you not applaud and adore me, sirs? why stand you mute? are you stupid? You are not worthy of the benefit.

DAUP: Did not I tell you? Mischief!—

CLER: I would you had placed this benefit somewhere else.
TRUE: Why so?

28

CLER: 'Slight, you have done the most inconsiderate, rash, weak thing, that ever man did to his friend.

DAUP: Friend! if the most malicious enemy I have, had studied to inflict an injury upon me, it could not be a greater.

TRUE: Wherein, for Gods-sake? Gentlemen, come to yourselves again.

DAUP: But I presaged thus much afore to you.

CLER: Would my lips had been solder'd when I spake on't. Slight, what moved you to be thus impertinent?

TRUE: My masters, do not put on this strange face to pay my courtesy; off with this visor. Have good turns done you, and thank 'em this way!

DAUP: 'Fore heav'n, you have undone me. That which I have plotted for, and been maturing now these four months, you have blasted in a minute: Now I am lost, I may speak. This gentlewoman was lodged here by me o' purpose, and, to be put upon my uncle, hath profest this obstinate silence for my sake; being my entire friend, and one that for the requital of such a fortune as to marry him, would have made me very ample conditions: where now, all my hopes are utterly miscarried by this unlucky accident.

CLER: Thus 'tis when a man will be ignorantly officious, do services, and not know his why; I wonder what courteous itch possest you. You never did absurder part in your life, nor a greater trespass to friendship or humanity.

DAUP: Faith, you may forgive it best: 'twas your cause principally.

CLER: I know it, would it had not.

[ENTER CUTBEARD.]

DAUP: How now, Cutbeard! what news?

CUT: The best, the happiest that ever was, sir. There has been a mad gentleman with your uncle, this morning,
[SEEING TRUEWIT.]

29

—I think this be the gentleman—that has almost talk'd him out of his wits, with threatening him from marriage—

DAUP: On, I prithee.

CUT: And your uncle, sir, he thinks 'twas done by your procurement; therefore he will see the party you wot of presently: and if he like her, he says, and that she be so inclining to dumb as I have told him, he swears he will marry her, to-day, instantly, and not defer it a minute longer.

DAUP: Excellent! beyond our expectation!

TRUE: Beyond our expectation! By this light, I knew it would be thus.

DAUP: Nay, sweet Truewit, forgive me.

TRUE: No, I was ignorantly officious, impertinent: this was the absurd, weak part.

CLER: Wilt thou ascribe that to merit now, was mere fortune?

TRUE: Fortune! mere providence. Fortune had not a finger in't. I saw it must necessarily in nature fall out so: my genius is never false to me in these things. Shew me how it could be otherwise.

DAUP: Nay, gentlemen, contend not, 'tis well now.

TRUE: Alas, I let him go on with inconsiderate, and rash, and what he pleas'd.

CLER: Away, thou strange justifier of thyself, to be wiser than thou wert, by the event!

TRUE: Event! by this light, thou shalt never persuade me, but I foresaw it as well as the stars themselves.

DAUP: Nay, gentlemen, 'tis well now. Do you two entertain sir John Daw with discourse, while I send her away with instructions.

TRUE: I will be acquainted with her first, by your favour.
CLER: Master True-wit, lady, a friend of ours.

TRUE: I am sorry I have not known you sooner, lady, to celebrate this rare virtue of your silence.

[EXEUNT DAUP., EPI., AND CUTBEARD.]

CLER: Faith, an you had come sooner, you should have seen and heard her well celebrated in sir John Daw's madrigals.

TRUE [ADVANCES TO DAW.]: Jack Daw, God save you! when saw you La-Foole?

DAW: Not since last night, master Truewit.

TRUE: That's a miracle! I thought you two had been inseparable.

DAW: He is gone to invite his guests.

TRUE: 'Odso! 'tis true! What a false memory have I towards that man! I am one: I met him even now, upon that he calls his delicate fine black horse, rid into a foam, with posting from place to place, and person to person, to give them the cue—

CLER: Lest they should forget?

TRUE: Yes: There was never poor captain took more pains at a muster to shew men, than he, at this meal, to shew friends.

DAW: It is his quarter-feast, sir.

CLER: What! do you say so, sir John?

TRUE: Nay, Jack Daw will not be out, at the best friends he has, to the talent of his wit: Where's his mistress, to hear and applaud him? is she gone?

DAW: Is mistress Epicoene gone?

CLER: Gone afore, with sir Dauphine, I warrant, to the place.

TRUE: Gone afore! that were a manifest injury; a disgrace and a half: to refuse him at such a festival-time as this, being a bravery, and a wit too!
CLER: Tut, he'll swallow it like cream: he's better read in Jure

civili, than to esteem any thing a disgrace, is offer'd him from a mistress.

DAW: Nay, let her e'en go; she shall sit alone, and be dumb in her chamber a week together, for John Daw, I warrant her. Does she refuse me?

CLER: No, sir, do not take it so to heart; she does not refuse you, but a little neglects you. Good faith, Truewit, you were to blame, to put it into his head, that she does refuse him.

TRUE: Sir, she does refuse him palpably, however you mince it. An I were as he, I would swear to speak ne'er a word to her to-day for't.

DAW: By this light, no more I will not.

TRUE: Nor to any body else, sir.

DAW: Nay, I will not say so, gentlemen.

CLER: It had been an excellent happy condition for the company, if you could have drawn him to it. [ASIDE.]

DAW: I'll be very melancholY, i'faith.

CLER: As a dog, if I were as you, sir John.

TRUE: Or a snail, or a hog-louse: I would roll myself up for this day, in troth, they should not unwind me.

DAW: By this pick-tooth, so I will.

CLER: 'Tis well done: He begins already to be angry with his teeth.

DAW: Will you go, gentlemen?

CLER: Nay, you must walk alone, if you be right melancholy, sir John.

TRUE: Yes, sir, we'll dog you, we'll follow you afar off.

[EXIT DAW.]

32

CLER: Was there ever such a two yards of knighthood measured out by time, to be sold to laughter?

TRUE: A mere talking mole, hang him! no mushroom was ever so fresh. A fellow so utterly nothing, as he knows not what he would be.

CLER: Let's follow him: but first, let's go to Dauphine, he's hovering about the house to hear what news.

TRUE: Content.

[EXEUNT.]

SCENE 2.3.

A ROOM IN MOROSE'S HOUSE.

ENTER MOROSE AND MUTE, FOLLOWED BY CUTBEARD WITH EPICOENE.

MOR: Welcome Cutbeard! draw near with your fair charge: and in her ear softly entreat her to unmasthey.
[EPI. TAKES OFF HER MASK.]
—So! Is the door shut?
[MUTE MAKES A LEG.]
—Enough. Now, Cutbeard, with the same discipline I use to my family, I will question you. As I conceive, Cutbeard, this gentlewoman is she you have provided, and brought, in hope she will fit me in the place and person of a wife? Answer me not, but with your leg, unless it be otherwise:
[CUT. MAKES A LEG.]
—Very well done, Cutbeard. I conceive, besides, Cutbeard, you have been pre-acquainted with her birth, education, and qualities, or else would not prefer her to my acceptance, in the weighty consequence of marriage.
[CUT. MAKES A LEG.]

33

—This I conceive, Cutbeard. Answer me not but with your leg, unless it be otherwise.
[CUT. BOWS AGAIN.]
—Very well done, Cutbeard. Give aside now a little, and leave me to examine her condition, and aptitude to my affection.
[HE GOES ABOUT HER, AND VIEWS HER.]
—She is exceeding fair, and of a special good favour; a sweet composition or harmony of limbs: her temper of beauty has the true height of my blood. The knave hath exceedingly well fitted me without: I will now try her within. Come near, fair gentlewoman: let not my behaviour seem rude, though unto you, being rare, it may haply appear strange.
[EPICOENE CURTSIES.]
—Nay, lady, you may speak, though Cutbeard and my man, might not;
for, of all sounds, only the sweet voice of a fair lady has the just length of mine ears. I beseech you, say, lady; out of the first fire of meeting eyes, they say, love is stricken: do you feel any such motion suddenly shot into you, from any part you see in me? ha, lady?
[EPICOENE CURTSIES.]
—Alas, lady, these answers by silent curtsies from you are too courtless and simple. I have ever had my breeding in court: and she that shall be my wife, must be accomplished with courtly and audacious ornaments. Can you speak, lady?

EPI: [softly.] Judge you, forsooth.

MOR: What say you, lady? speak out, I beseech you.

EPI: Judge you, forsooth.

MOR: On my judgment, a divine softness! But can you naturally, lady, as I enjoin these by doctrine and industry, refer yourself to the search of my judgment, and, not taking pleasure in your tongue, which is a woman's chiefest pleasure, think it plausible to answer me by silent gestures, so long as my speeches jump right with what you conceive?
[EPI. CURTSIES.]
—Excellent! divine! if it were possible she should hold out thus! Peace, Cutbeard, thou art made for ever, as thou hast made me, if this felicity have lasting: but I will try her further. Dear lady, I am courtly, I tell you, and I must have mine ears banqueted with pleasant and witty conferences, pretty girls, scoffs, and

dalliance in her that I mean to choose for my bed-phere. The
ladies in court think it a most desperate impair to their
quickness of wit, and good carriage, if they cannot give
occasion for a man to court 'em; and when an amorous discourse
is set on foot, minister as good matter to continue it, as himself:
And do you alone so much differ from all them, that what they,
with so much circumstance, affect and toil for, to seem
learn'd, to seem judicious, to seem sharp and conceited, you
can bury in yourself with silence, and rather trust your graces
to the fair conscience of virtue, than to the world's or your own
proclamation?

EPI [SOFTLY]: I should be sorry else.

MOR: What say you lady? good lady, speak out.

EPI: I should be sorry else.

MOR: That sorrow doth fill me with gladness. O Morose, thou art
happy above mankind! pray that thou mayest contain thyself. I
will only put her to it once more, and it shall be with the utmost
touch and test of their sex. But hear me, fair lady; I do also
love to see her whom I shall choose for my heifer, to be the
first and principal in all fashions; precede all the dames at
court by a fortnight; have council of tailors, lineners,
lace-women, embroiderers, and sit with them sometimes twice a
day upon French intelligences; and then come forth varied like
nature, or oftener than she, and better by the help of art, her
emulous servant. This do I affect: and how will you be able, lady,
with this frugality of speech, to give the manifold but
necessary instructions, for that bodice, these sleeves, those
skirts, this cut, that stitch, this embroidery, that lace, this
wire, those knots, that ruff, those roses, this girdle, that
fanne, the t'other scarf, these gloves? Ha! what say you, lady?

EPI [SOFTLY]: I'll leave it to you, sir.

MOR: How, lady? pray you rise a note.

EPI: I leave it to wisdom and you, sir.

MOR: Admirable creature! I will trouble you no more: I will not
sin against so sweet a simplicity. Let me now be bold to print on
those divine lips the seal of being mine.—Cutbeard, I give thee

the lease of thy house free: thank me not but with thy leg
[CUTBEARD SHAKES HIS HEAD.]
—I know what thou wouldst say, she's poor, and her friends
deceased. She has brought a wealthy dowry in her silence,
Cutbeard; and in respect of her poverty, Cutbeard, I shall have her
more loving and obedient, Cutbeard. Go thy ways, and get me a
minister presently, with a soft low voice, to marry us; and pray
him he will not be impertinent, but brief as he can; away: softly,
[EXIT CUTBEARD.]
—Sirrah, conduct your mistress into the dining-room, your now
mistress.
[EXIT MUTE, FOLLOWED BY EPI.]
—O my felicity! how I shall be revenged on mine insolent kinsman,
and his plots to fright me from marrying! This night I will get an
heir, and thrust him out of my blood, like a stranger; he would be
knighted, forsooth, and thought by that means to reign over me;
his title must do it: No, kinsman, I will now make you bring me
the tenth lord's and the sixteenth lady's letter, kinsman; and it
shall do you no good, kinsman. Your knighthood itself shall come
on its knees, and it shall be rejected; it shall be sued for its
fees to execution, and not be redeem'd; it shall cheat at the
twelvepenny ordinary, it knighthood, for its diet, all the term-
time, and tell tales for it in the vacation to the hostess; or it
knighthood shall do worse, take sanctuary in Cole-harbour, and
fast. It shall fright all its friends with borrowing letters; and when
one of the fourscore hath brought it knighthood ten shillings, it
knighthood shall go to the Cranes, or the Bear at the Bridge-foot,
and be drunk in fear: it shall not have money to discharge one
tavern-reckoning, to invite the old creditors to forbear it
knighthood, or the new, that should be, to trust it knighthood. It
shall be the tenth name in the bond to take up the commodity of
pipkins and stone jugs: and the part thereof shall not furnish it
knighthood forth for the attempting of a baker's widow, a brown
baker's widow. It shall give it knighthood's name, for a stallion,
to all gamesome citizens' wives, and be refused; when the master
of a dancing school, or how do you call him, the worst reveller in
the town is taken: it shall want clothes, and by reason of that,
wit, to fool to lawyers. It shall not have hope to repair itself
by Constantinople, Ireland, or Virginia; but the best and last
fortune to it knighthood shall be to make Dol Tear-Sheet, or Kate
Common a lady: and so it knighthood may eat.

[EXIT.]

SCENE 2.4.

A LANE, NEAR MOROSE'S HOUSE.

ENTER TRUEWIT, DAUPHINE,AND CLERIMONT.

TRUE: Are you sure he is not gone by?

DAUP: No, I staid in the shop ever since.

CLER: But he may take the other end of the lane.

DAUP: No, I told him I would be here at this end: I appointed him hither.

TRUE: What a barbarian it is to stay then!

DAUP: Yonder he comes.

CLER: And his charge left behind him, which is a very good sign, Dauphine.

[ENTER CUTBEARD.]

DAUP: How now Cutbeard! succeeds it, or no?

CUT: Past imagination, sir, omnia secunda; you could not have pray'd to have had it so well. Saltat senex, as it is in the proverb; he does triumph in his felicity, admires the party! he has given me the lease of my house too! and I am now going for a silent minister to marry them, and away.

TRUE: 'Slight, get one of the silenced ministers, a zealous brother would torment him purely.

CUT: Cum privilegio, sir.

DAUP: O, by no means, let's do nothing to hinder it now: when it is done and finished, I am for you, for any device of vexation.

CUT: And that shall be within this half hour, upon my dexterity, gentlemen. Contrive what you can in the mean time, bonis avibus.

37

[EXIT.]

CLER: How the slave doth Latin it!

TRUE: It would be made a jest to posterity, sirs, this day's mirth, if ye will.

CLER: Beshrew his heart that will not, I pronounce.

DAUP: And for my part. What is it?

TRUE: To translate all La-Foole's company, and his feast thither, to-day, to celebrate this bride-ale.

DAUP: Ay marry; but how will't be done?

TRUE: I'll undertake the directing of all the lady-guests thither, and then the meat must follow.

CLER: For God's sake, let's effect it: it will be an excellent comedy of affliction, so many several noises.

DAUP: But are they not at the other place already, think you?

TRUE: I'll warrant you for the college-honours: one of their faces has not the priming colour laid on yet, nor the other her smock sleek'd.

CLER: O, but they'll rise earlier then ordinary, to a feast.

TRUE: Best go see, and assure ourselves.

CLER: Who knows the house?

TRUE: I will lead you: Were you never there yet?

DAUP: Not I.

CLER: Nor I.

TRUE: Where have you lived then? not know Tom Otter!

CLER: No: for God's sake, what is he?

TRUE: An excellent animal, equal with your Daw or La-Foole, if not transcendant; and does Latin it as much as your barber: He is his wife's subject, he calls her princess, and at such times as these follows her up and down the house like a page, with his hat off, partly for heat, partly for reverence. At this instant he is marshalling of his bull, bear, and horse.

DAUP: What be those, in the name of Sphynx?

TRUE: Why, sir, he has been a great man at the Bear-garden in his time; and from that subtle sport, has ta'en the witty denomination of his chief carousing cups. One he calls his bull, another his bear, another his horse. And then he has his lesser glasses, that he calls his deer and his ape; and several degrees of them too; and never is well, nor thinks any entertainment perfect, till these be brought out, and set on the cupboard.

CLER: For God's love!—we should miss this, if we should not go.

TRUE: Nay, he has a thousand things as good, that will speak him all day. He will rail on his wife, with certain common places, behind her back; and to her face—

DAUP: No more of him. Let's go see him, I petition you.

[EXEUNT.]

ACT 3.

SCENE 3.1.

A ROOM IN OTTER'S HOUSE.

ENTER CAPTAIN OTTER WITH HIS CUPS, AND MISTRESS OTTER.

OTT: Nay, good princess, hear me pauca verba.

MRS. OTT: By that light, I'll have you chain'd up, with your bull-dogs, and bear-dogs, if you be not civil the sooner. I will send you to kennel, i'faith. You were best bait me with your bull, bear, and horse! Never a time that the courtiers or collegiates come to the house, but you make it a Shrove-tuesday! I would have you get your Whitsuntide velvet cap, and your staff in your hand, to entertain them: yes, in troth, do.

OTT: Not so, princess, neither; but under correction, sweet princess, give me leave.—These things I am known to the courtiers by: It is reported to them for my humour, and they receive it so, and do expect it. Tom Otter's bull, bear, and horse is known all over England, in rerum natura.

MRS. OTT: 'Fore me, I will na-ture them over to Paris-garden, and na-ture you thither too, if you pronounce them again. Is a bear a fit beast, or a bull, to mix in society with great ladies? think in your discretion, in any good policy.

OTT: The horse then, good princess.

MRS. OTT: Well, I am contented for the horse: they love to be well horsed, I know. I love it myself.

OTT: And it is a delicate fine horse this. Poetarum Pegasus. Under correction, princess, Jupiter did turn himself into a—taurus, or bull, under correction, good princess.

[ENTER TRUEWIT, CLERIMONT, AND DAUPHINE, BEHIND.]

MRS. OTT: By my integrity, I will send you over to the Bank-side, I will commit you to the master of the Garden, if I hear but a syllable more. Must my house or my roof be polluted with the scent of bears and bulls, when it is perfumed for great ladies? Is this according to the instrument, when I married you? that I would be princess, and reign in mine own house: and you would be my subject, and obey me? What did you bring me, should make you thus peremptory? do I allow you your half-crown a day, to spend where you will, among your gamsters, to vex and torment me at such times as these? Who gives you your maintenance, I pray you? who allows you your horse-meat and man's meat? your three suits of apparel a year? your four pair of stockings, one silk, three worsted? your clean linen, your bands and cuffs, when I can get you to wear them?—'tis marle you have them on now.—Who graces you with courtiers or great personages, to speak to you out of their coaches, and come home to your house? Were you ever so much as look'd upon by a lord or a lady, before I married you, but on the Easter or Whitsun-holidays? and then out at the banquetting-house window, when Ned Whiting or George Stone were at the stake?

TRUE: For Gods sake, let's go stave her off him.

MRS. OTT: Answer me to that. And did not I take you up from thence, in an old greasy buff-doublet, with points, and green velvet sleeves, out at the elbows? you forget this.

TRUE: She'll worry him, if we help not in time.

[THEY COME FORWARD.]

MRS. OTT: O, here are some of the gallants! Go to, behave yourself distinctly, and with good morality: or, I protest, I will take away your exhibition.

TRUE: By your leave, fair mistress Otter, I will be bold to enter these gentlemen in your acquaintance.

MRS. OTT: It shall not be obnoxious, or difficil, sir.

TRUE: How does my noble captain? is the bull, bear, and horse in rerum natura still?

OTT: Sir, sic visum superis.

41

MRS. OTT: I would you would but intimate them, do. Go your ways in, and get toasts and butter made for the woodcocks. That's a fit province for you.

[DRIVES HIM OFF.]

CLER: Alas, what a tyranny is this poor fellow married to!

TRUE: O, but the sport will be anon, when we get him loose.

DAUP: Dares he ever speak?

TRUE: No Anabaptist ever rail'd with the like license: but mark her language in the mean time, I beseech you.

MRS. OTT: Gentlemen, you are very aptly come. My cousin, sir Amorous, will be here briefly.

TRUE: In good time lady. Was not sir John Daw here, to ask for him, and the company?

MRS. OTT: I cannot assure you, master Truewit. Here was a very melancholy knight in a ruff, that demanded my subject for somebody, a gentleman, I think.

CLER: Ay, that was he, lady.

MRS. OTT: But he departed straight, I can resolve you.

DAUP: What an excellent choice phrase this lady expresses in.

TRUE: O, sir, she is the only authentical courtier, that is not naturally bred one, in the city.

MRS. OTT: You have taken that report upon trust, gentlemen.

TRUE: No, I assure you, the court governs it so, lady, in your behalf.

MRS. OTT: I am the servant of the court and courtiers, sir.

TRUE: They are rather your idolaters.

MRS. OTT: Not so, sir.

42

[ENTER CUTBEARD.]

DAUP: How now, Cutbeard? any cross?

CUT: O, no, sir, omnia bene. 'Twas never better on the hinges; all's sure. I have so pleased him with a curate, that he's gone to't almost with the delight he hopes for soon.

DAUP: What is he for a vicar?

CUT: One that has catch'd a cold, sir, and can scarce be heard six inches off; as if he spoke out of a bulrush that were not pick'd, or his throat were full of pith: a fine quick fellow, and an excellent barber of prayers. I came to tell you, sir, that you might omnem movere lapidem, as they say, be ready with your vexation.

DAUP: Gramercy, honest Cutbeard! be thereabouts with thy key, to let us in.

CUT: I will not fail you, sir: ad manum.

[EXIT.]

TRUE: Well, I'll go watch my coaches.

CLER: Do; and we'll send Daw to you, if you meet him not.

[EXIT TRUEWIT.]

MRS. OTT: Is master Truewit gone?

DAUP: Yes, lady, there is some unfortunate business fallen out.

MRS. OTT: So I adjudged by the physiognomy of the fellow that came in; and I had a dream last night too of a new pageant, and my lady mayoress, which is always very ominous to me. I told it my lady Haughty t'other day; when her honour came hither to see some China stuffs: and she expounded it out of Artemidorus, and I have found it since very true. It has done me many affronts.

CLER: Your dream, lady?

MRS. OTT: Yes, sir, any thing I do but dream of the city. It

43

stain'd me a damasque table-cloth, cost me eighteen pound, at one time; and burnt me a black satin gown, as I stood by the fire, at my lady Centaure's chamber in the college, another time. A third time, at the lord's masque, it dropt all my wire and my ruff with wax candle, that I could not go up to the banquet. A fourth time, as I was taking coach to go to Ware, to meet a friend, it dash'd me a new suit all over (a crimson satin doublet, and black velvet skirts) with a brewer's horse, that I was fain to go in and shift me, and kept my chamber a leash of days for the anguish of it.

DAUP: These were dire mischances, lady.

CLER: I would not dwell in the city, an 'twere so fatal to me.

MRS. OTT: Yes sir, but I do take advice of my doctor to dream of it as little as I can.

DAUP: You do well, mistress Otter.

MRS. OTT: Will it please you to enter the house farther, gentlemen?

DAUP: And your favour, lady: but we stay to speak with a knight, sir John Daw, who is here come. We shall follow you, lady.

MRS. OTT: At your own time, sir. It is my cousin sir Amorous his feast—

DAUP: I know it, lady.

MRS. OTT: And mine together. But it is for his honour, and therefore I take no name of it, more than of the place.

DAUP: You are a bounteous kinswoman.

MRS. OTT: Your servant, sir.

[EXIT.]

CLER [COMING FORWARD WITH DAW.]: Why, do not you know it, sir John Daw?

DAW: No, I am a rook if I do.

44

CLER: I'll tell you then, she's married by this time. And, whereas you were put in the head, that she was gone with sir Dauphine, I assure you, sir Dauphine has been the noblest, honestest friend to you, that ever gentleman of your quality could boast of. He has discover'd the whole plot, and made your mistress so acknowledging, and indeed so ashamed of her injury to you, that she desires you to forgive her, and but grace her wedding with your presence to-day—She is to be married to a very good fortune, she says, his uncle, old Morose: and she will'd me in private to tell you, that she shall be able to do you more favours, and with more security now, than before.

DAW: Did she say so, i'faith?

CLER: Why, what do you think of me, sir John? ask sir Dauphine.

DAUP: Nay, I believe you.—Good sir Dauphine, did she desire me to forgive her?

CLER: I assure you, sir John, she did.

DAW: Nay, then, I do with all my heart, and I'll be jovial.

CLER: Yes, for look you, sir, this was the injury to you. La-Foole intended this feast to honour her bridal day, and made you the property to invite the college ladies, and promise to bring her: and then at the time she should have appear'd, as his friend, to have given you the dor. Whereas now, Sir Dauphine has brought her to a feeling of it, with this kind of satisfaction, that you shall bring all the ladies to the place where she is, and be very jovial; and there, she will have a dinner, which shall be in your name: and so disappoint La-Foole, to make you good again, and, as it were, a saver in the main.

DAW: As I am a knight, I honour her; and forgive her heartily.

CLER: About it then presently. Truewit is gone before to confront the coaches, and to acquaint you with so much, if he meet you. Join with him, and 'tis well.—
[ENTER SIR AMOROUS LAFOOLE.]
See; here comes your antagonist, but take you no notice, but be very jovial.
LA-F: Are the ladies come, sir John Daw, and your mistress?

[EXIT DAW.]

—Sir Dauphine! you are exceeding welcome, and honest master
Clerimont. Where's my cousin? did you see no collegiates,
gentlemen?

DAUP: Collegiates! do you not hear, sir Amorous, how you are
abus'd?

LA-F: How, sir!

CLER: Will you speak so kindly to sir John Daw, that has done you
such an affront?

LA-F: Wherein, gentlemen? let me be a suitor to you to know, I
beseech you!

CLER: Why, sir, his mistress is married to-day to sir Dauphine's
uncle, your cousin's neighbour, and he has diverted all the ladies,
and all your company thither, to frustrate your provision, and
stick a disgrace upon you. He was here now to have enticed us
away from you too: but we told him his own, I think.

LA-F: Has sir John Daw wrong'd me so inhumanly?

DAUP: He has done it, sir Amorous, most maliciously and
treacherously: but, if youll be ruled by us, you shall quit him,
i'faith.

LA-F: Good gentlemen, I'll make one, believe it. How, I pray?

DAUP: Marry sir, get me your pheasants, and your godwits, and
your best meat, and dish it in silver dishes of your cousin's
presently, and say nothing, but clap me a clean towel about you,
like a sewer; and bare-headed, march afore it with a good
confidence, ('tis but
over the way, hard by,) and we'll second you, where you shall set
it on the board, and bid them welcome to't, which shall shew 'tis
yours, and disgrace his preparation utterly: and, for your cousin,
whereas she should be troubled here at home with care of making
and giving welcome, she shall transfer all that labour thither, and
be a principal guest herself, sit rank'd with the college-honours,
and be honour'd, and have her health drunk as often, as bare and
as loud as the best of them.

LA-F: I'll go tell her presently. It shall be done, that's resolved.

[EXIT.]

CLER: I thought he would not hear it out, but 'twould take him.

DAUP: Well, there be guests and meat now; how shall we do for music?

CLER: The smell of the venison, going through the street, will invite one noise of fiddlers or other.

DAUP: I would it would call the trumpeters hither!

CLER: Faith, there is hope: they have intelligence of all feasts. There's good correspondence betwixt them and the London cooks: 'tis twenty to one but we have them.

DAUP: 'Twill be a most solemn day for my uncle, and an excellent fit of mirth for us.

CLER: Ay, if we can hold up the emulation betwixt Foole and Daw, and never bring them to expostulate.

DAUP: Tut, flatter them both, as Truewit says, and you may take their understandings in a purse-net. They'll believe themselves to be just such men as we make them, neither more nor less. They have nothing, not the use of their senses, but by tradition.

[RE-ENTER LA-FOOLE, LIKE A SEWER.]

CLER: See! sir Amorous has his towel on already. Have you persuaded your cousin?

LA-F: Yes, 'tis very feasible: she'll do any thing she says, rather than the La-Fooles shall be disgraced.

DAUP: She is a noble kinswoman. It will be such a pestling device, sir Amorous; it will pound all your enemy's practices to powder, and blow him up with his own mine, his own train.

LA-F: Nay, we'll give fire, I warrant you.

CLER: But you must carry it privately, without any noise, and take no notice by any means—

[RE-ENTER CAPTAIN OTTER.]

OTT: Gentlemen, my princess says you shall have all her silver dishes, festinate: and she's gone to alter her tire a little, and go with you—

CLER: And yourself too, captain Otter?

DAUP: By any means, sir.

OTT: Yes, sir, I do mean it: but I would entreat my cousin sir Amorous, and you, gentlemen, to be suitors to my princess, that I may carry my bull and my bear, as well as my horse.

CLER: That you shall do, captain Otter.

LA-F: My cousin will never consent, gentlemen.

DAUP: She must consent, sir Amorous, to reason.

LA-F: Why, she says they are no decorum among ladies.

OTT: But they are decora, and that's better, sir.

CLER: Ay, she must hear argument. Did not Pasiphae, who was a queen, love a bull? and was not Calisto, the mother of Arcas, turn'd into a bear, and made a star, mistress Ursula, in the heavens?

OTT: O lord! that I could have said as much! I will have these stories painted in the Bear-garden, ex Ovidii metamorphosi.

DAUP: Where is your princess, captain? pray, be our leader.

OTT: That I shall, sir.

CLER: Make haste, good sir Amorous.

[EXEUNT.]

48

SCENE 3.2.

A ROOM IN MOROSE'S HOUSE.

ENTER MOROSE, EPICOENE, PARSON, AND CUTBEARD.

MOR: Sir, there is an angel for yourself, and a brace of angels for your cold. Muse not at this manage of my bounty. It is fit we should thank fortune, double to nature, for any benefit she confers upon us; besides, it is your imperfection, but my solace.

PAR [SPEAKS AS HAVING A COLD.] I thank your worship; so is it mine, now.

MOR: What says he, Cutbeard?

CUT: He says, praesto, sir, whensoever your worship needs him, he can be ready with the like. He got this cold with sitting up late, and singing catches with cloth-workers.

MOR: No more. I thank him.

PAR: God keep your worship, and give you much joy with your fair spouse.—[COUGHS.] uh! uh! uh!

MOR: O, O! stay Cutbeard! let him give me five shillings of my money back. As it is bounty to reward benefits, so is it equity to mulct injuries. I will have it. What says he?

CUT: He cannot change it, sir.

MOR: It must be changed.

CUT [ASIDE TO PARSON.]: Cough again.

MOR: What says he?

CUT: He will cough out the rest, sir.

PAR: Uh, uh, uh!

MOR: Away, away with him! stop his mouth! away! I forgive it.—

49

[EXIT CUT. THRUSTING OUT THE PAR.]

EPI: Fie, master Morose, that you will use this violence to a man of the church.

MOR: How!

EPI: It does not become your gravity, or breeding, as you pretend, in court, to have offer'd this outrage on a waterman, or any more boisterous creature, much less on a man of his civil coat.

MOR: You can speak then!

EPI: Yes, sir.

MOR: Speak out, I mean.

EPI: Ay, sir. Why, did you think you had married a statue, or a motion, only? one of the French puppets, with the eyes turn'd with a wire? or some innocent out of the hospital, that would stand with her hands thus, and a plaise mouth, and look upon you?

MOR: O immodesty! a manifest woman! What, Cutbeard!

EPI: Nay, never quarrel with Cutbeard, sir; it is too late now. I confess it doth bate somewhat of the modesty I had, when I writ simply maid: but I hope, I shall make it a stock still competent to the estate and dignity of your wife.

MOR: She can talk!

EPI: Yes, indeed, sir.

[ENTER MUTE.]

MOR: What sirrah! None of my knaves there? where is this impostor, Cutbeard?

[MUTE MAKES SIGNS.]

EPI: Speak to him, fellow, speak to him! I'll have none of this coacted, unnatural dumbness in my house, in a family where I govern.

50

[EXIT MUTE.]

MOR: She is my regent already! I have married a Penthesilea, a Semiramis, sold my liberty to a distaff.

[ENTER TRUEWIT.]

TRUE: Where's master Morose?

MOR: Is he come again! Lord have mercy upon me!

TRUE: I wish you all joy, mistress Epicoene, with your grave and honourable match.

EPI: I return you the thanks, master Truewit, so friendly a wish deserves.

MOR: She has acquaintance, too!

TRUE: God save you, sir, and give you all contentment in your fair choice, here! Before, I was the bird of night to you, the owl; but now I am the messenger of peace, a dove, and bring you the glad wishes of many friends to the celebration of this good hour.

MOR: What hour, sir?

TRUE: Your marriage hour, sir. I commend your resolution, that, notwithstanding all the dangers I laid afore you, in the voice of a night-crow, would yet go on, and be yourself. It shews you are a man constant to your own ends, and upright to your purposes, that would not be put off with left-handed cries.

MOR: How should you arrive at the knowledge of so much!

TRUE: Why, did you ever hope, sir, committing the secrecy of it to a barber, that less then the whole town should know it? you might as well have told it the conduit, or the bake-house, or the infantry that follow the court, and with more security. Could your gravity forget so old and noted a remnant, as lippis et tonsoribus notum? Well, sir, forgive it yourself now, the fault, and be communicable with your friends. Here will be three or four fashionable ladies from the college to visit you presently, and their train of minions and followers.

51

MOR: Bar my doors! bar my doors! Where are all my eaters? my mouths now?—
[ENTER SERVANTS.]
Bar up my doors, you varlets!

EPI: He is a varlet that stirs to such an office. Let them stand open. I would see him that dares move his eyes toward it. Shall I have a barricado made against my friends, to be barr'd of any pleasure they can bring in to me with their honourable visitation?

[EXEUNT SER.]

MOR: O Amazonian impudence!

TRUE: Nay, faith, in this, sir, she speaks but reason: and, methinks, is more continent than you. Would you go to bed so presently, sir, afore noon? a man of your head and hair should owe more to that reverend ceremony, and not mount the marriage-bed like a town-bull, or a mountain-goat; but stay the due season; and ascend it then with religion and fear. Those delights are to be steeped in the humour and silence of the night; and give the day to other open pleasures, and jollities of feasting, of music, of revels, of discourse: we'll have all, sir, that may make your Hymen high and happy.

MOR: O, my torment, my torment!

TRUE: Nay, if you endure the first half hour, sir, so tediously, and with this irksomness; what comfort or hope can this fair gentlewoman make to herself hereafter, in the consideration of so many years as are to come—

MOR: Of my affliction. Good sir, depart, and let her do it alone.

TRUE: I have done, sir.

MOR: That cursed barber.

TRUE: Yes, faith, a cursed wretch indeed, sir.

MOR: I have married his cittern, that's common to all men. Some plague above the plague—

52

TRUE: All Egypt's ten plagues.

MOR: Revenge me on him!

TRUE: 'Tis very well, sir. If you laid on a curse or two more,
I'll assure you he'll bear them. As, that he may get the pox
with seeking to cure it, sir; or, that while he is curling another
man's hair, his own may drop off; or, for burning some male-
bawd's lock, he may have his brain beat out with the curling-iron.

MOR: No, let the wretch live wretched. May he get the itch, and
his shop so lousy, as no man dare come at him, nor he come at no
man!

TRUE: Ay, and if he would swallow all his balls for pills, let not
them purge him.

MOR: Let his warming pan be ever cold.

TRUE: A perpetual frost underneath it, sir.

MOR: Let him never hope to see fire again.

TRUE: But in hell, sir.

MOR: His chairs be always empty, his scissors rust, and his combs
mould in their cases.

TRUE: Very dreadful that! And may he lose the invention, sir, of
carving lanterns in paper.

MOR: Let there be no bawd carted that year, to employ a bason of
his: but let him be glad to eat his sponge for bread.

TRUE: And drink lotium to it, and much good do him.

MOR: Or, for want of bread—

TRUE: Eat ear-wax, sir. I'll help you. Or, draw his own teeth,
and add them to the lute-string.

MOR: No, beat the old ones to powder, and make bread of them.

TRUE: Yes, make meal of the mill-stones.

MOR: May all the botches and burns that he has cured on others break out upon him.

TRUE: And he now forget the cure of them in himself, sir: or, if he do remember it, let him have scraped all his linen into lint for't, and have not a rag left him to set up with.

MOR: Let him never set up again, but have the gout in his hands for ever! Now, no more, sir.

TRUE: O, that last was too high set; you might go less with him, i'faith, and be revenged enough: as, that he be never able to new-paint his pole—

MOR: Good sir, no more, I forgot myself.

TRUE: Or, want credit to take up with a comb-maker—

MOR: No more, sir.

TRUE: Or, having broken his glass in a former despair, fall now into a much greater, of ever getting another—

MOR: I beseech you, no more.

TRUE: Or, that he never be trusted with trimming of any but chimney-sweepers—

MOR: Sir—

TRUE: Or, may he cut a collier's throat with his razor, by chance-medley, and yet be hanged for't.

MOR: I will forgive him, rather than hear any more. I beseech you, sir.

[ENTER DAW, INTRODUCING LADY HAUGHTY, CENTAURE, MAVIS, AND TRUSTY.]

DAW: This way, madam.

MOR: O, the sea breaks in upon me! another flood! an inundation! I shall be overwhelmed with noise. It beats already at my shores. I feel an earthquake in my self for't.

DAW: 'Give you joy, mistress.

MOR: Has she servants too!

DAW: I have brought some ladies here to see and know you.
My lady Haughty—
[AS HE PRESENTS THEM SEVERALLY, EPI. KISSES THEM.]
this my lady Centaure—mistress Dol Mavis—mistress Trusty,
my lady Haughty's woman. Where's your husband? let's see him:
can he endure no noise? let me come to him.

MOR: What nomenclator is this!

TRUE: Sir John Daw, sir, your wife's servant, this.

MOR: A Daw, and her servant! O, 'tis decreed, 'tis decreed of me,
an she have such servants.

TRUE: Nay sir, you must kiss the ladies; you must not go away,
now: they come toward you to seek you out.

HAU: I'faith, master Morose, would you steal a marriage thus, in
the midst of so many friends, and not acquaint us? Well, I'll kiss
you, notwithstanding the justice of my quarrel: you shall give me
leave, mistress, to use a becoming familiarity with your husband.

EPI: Your ladyship does me an honour in it, to let me know he is
so worthy your favour: as you have done both him and me grace to
visit so unprepared a pair to entertain you.

MOR: Compliment! compliment!

EPI: But I must lay the burden of that upon my servant here.

HAU: It shall not need, mistress Morose, we will all bear, rather
than one shall be opprest.

MOR: I know it: and you will teach her the faculty, if she be to
learn it.

[WALKS ASIDE WHILE THE REST TALK APART.]

HAU: Is this the silent woman?

CEN: Nay, she has found her tongue since she was married, master Truewit says.

HAU: O, master Truewit! 'save you. What kind of creature is your bride here? she speaks, methinks!

TRUE: Yes, madam, believe it, she is a gentlewoman of very absolute behaviour, and of a good race.

HAU: And Jack Daw told us she could not speak!

TRUE: So it was carried in plot, madam, to put her upon this old fellow, by sir Dauphine, his nephew, and one or two more of us: but she is a woman of an excellent assurance, and an extraordinary happy wit and tongue. You shall see her make rare sport with Daw ere night.

HAU: And he brought us to laugh at her!

TRUE: That falls out often, madam, that he that thinks himself the master-wit, is the master-fool. I assure your ladyship, ye cannot laugh at her.

HAU: No, we'll have her to the college: An she have wit, she shall be one of us, shall she not Centaure? we'll make her a collegiate.

CEN: Yes faith, madam, and mistress Mavis and she will set up a side.

TRUE: Believe it, madam, and mistress Mavis she will sustain her part.

MAV: I'll tell you that, when I have talk'd with her, and tried her.

HAU: Use her very civilly, Mavis.

MAV: So I will, madam.

[WHISPERS HER.]

MOR: Blessed minute! that they would whisper thus ever!

56

[ASIDE.]

TRUE: In the mean time, madam, would but your ladyship help to vex him a little: you know his disease, talk to him about the wedding ceremonies, or call for your gloves, or—

HAU: Let me alone. Centaure, help me. Master bridegroom, where are you?

MOR: O, it was too miraculously good to last!

[ASIDE.]

HAU: We see no ensigns of a wedding here; no character of a bride-ale: where be our scarves and our gloves? I pray you, give them us. Let us know your bride's colours, and yours at least.

CEN: Alas, madam, he has provided none.

MOR: Had I known your ladyship's painter, I would.

HAU: He has given it you, Centaure, i'faith. But do you hear, master Morose? a jest will not absolve you in this manner. You that have suck'd the milk of the court, and from thence have been brought up to the very strong meats and wine, of it; been a courtier from the biggen to the night-cap, as we may say, and you to offend in such a high point of ceremony as this, and let your nuptials want all marks of solemnity! How much plate have you lost to-day, (if you had but regarded your profit,) what gifts, what friends, through your mere rusticity!

MOR: Madam—

HAU: Pardon me, sir, I must insinuate your errors to you; no gloves? no garters? no scarves? no epithalamium? no masque?

DAW: Yes, madam, I'll make an epithalamium, I promise my mistress; I have begun it already: will you ladyship hear it?

HAU: Ay, good Jack Daw.

MOR: Will it please your ladyship command a chamber, and be private with your friend? you shall have your choice of rooms to retire to after: my whole house is yours. I know it hath been your ladyship's errand into the city at other times, however now you have been unhappily diverted upon me: but I shall be loth to break any honourable custom of your ladyship's. And therefore, good madam—

EPI: Come, you are a rude bridegroom, to entertain ladies of honour in this fashion.

CEN: He is a rude groom indeed.

TRUE: By that light you deserve to be grafted, and have your horns reach from one side of the island, to the other. Do not mistake me, sir; I but speak this to give the ladies some heart again, not for any malice to you.

MOR: Is this your bravo, ladies?

TRUE: As God [shall] help me, if you utter such another word, I'll take mistress bride in, and begin to you in a very sad cup; do you see? Go to, know your friends, and such as love you.

[ENTER CLERIMONT, FOLLOWED BY A NUMBER OF MUSICIANS.]

CLER: By your leave, ladies. Do you want any music? I have brought you variety of noises. Play, sirs, all of you.

[ASIDE TO THE MUSICIANS, WHO STRIKE UP ALL TOGETHER.]

MOR: O, a plot, a plot, a plot, a plot, upon me! this day I shall be their anvil to work on, they will grate me asunder. 'Tis worse then the noise of a saw.

CLER: No, they are hair, rosin, and guts. I can give you the receipt.

TRUE: Peace, boys!

CLER: Play! I say.

TRUE: Peace, rascals! You see who's your friend now, sir: take courage, put on a martyr's resolution. Mock down all their attemptings with patience: 'tis but a day, and I would suffer

58

heroically. Should an ass exceed me in fortitude? no. You betray your infirmity with your hanging dull ears, and make them insult: bear up bravely, and constantly.
[LA-FOOLE PASSES OVER THE STAGE AS A SEWER, FOLLOWED BY SERVANTS CARRYING DISHES, AND MISTRESS OTTER.]
—Look you here, sir, what honour is done you unexpected, by your nephew; a wedding-dinner come, and a knight-sewer before it, for the more reputation: and fine mistress Otter, your neighbour, in the rump, or tail of it.

MOR: Is that Gorgon, that Medusa come! hide me, hide me.

TRUE: I warrant you, sir, she will not transform you. Look upon her with a good courage. Pray you entertain her, and conduct your guests in. No!—Mistress bride, will you entreat in the ladies? your bride-groom is so shame-faced, here.

EPI: Will it please your ladyship, madam?

HAU: With the benefit of your company, mistress.

EPI: Servant, pray you perform your duties.

DAW: And glad to be commanded, mistress.

CEN: How like you her wit, Mavis?

MAV: Very prettily, absolutely well.

MRS. OTT: 'Tis my place.

MAV: You shall pardon me, mistress Otter.

MRS. OTT: Why, I am a collegiate.

MAV: But not in ordinary.

MRS. OTT: But I am.

MAV: We'll dispute that within.

[EXEUNT LADIES.]

CLER: Would this had lasted a little longer.

TRUE: And that they had sent for the heralds.
[ENTER CAPTAIN OTTER.]
—Captain Otter! what news?

OTT: I have brought my bull, bear, and horse, in private, and yonder are the trumpeters without, and the drum, gentlemen.

[THE DRUM AND TRUMPETS SOUND WITHIN.]

MOR: O, O, O!

OTT: And we will have a rouse in each of them, anon, for bold Britons, i'faith.

[THEY SOUND AGAIN.]

MOR: O, O, O!
[EXIT HASTILY.]

OMNES: Follow, follow, follow!

ACT 4

SCENE 4.1.

A ROOM IN MOROSE'S HOUSE.

ENTER TRUEWIT AND CLERIMONT.

TRUE: Was there ever poor bridegroom so tormented? or man, indeed?

CLER: I have not read of the like in the chronicles of the land.

TRUE: Sure, he cannot but go to a place of rest, after all this purgatory.

CLER: He may presume it, I think.

TRUE: The spitting, the coughing, the laughter, the neezing, the farting, dancing, noise of the music, and her masculine and loud commanding, and urging the whole family, makes him think he has married a fury.

CLER: And she carries it up bravely.

TRUE: Ay, she takes any occasion to speak: that is the height on't.

CLER: And how soberly Dauphine labours to satisfy him, that it was none of his plot!

TRUE: And has almost brought him to the faith, in the article.
Here he comes.
[ENTER SIR DAUPHINE.]
—Where is he now? what's become of him, Dauphine?

DAUP: O, hold me up a little, I shall go away in the jest else. He has got on his whole nest of night-caps, and lock'd himself up in the top of the house, as high as ever he can climb from the noise. I peep'd in at a cranny, and saw him sitting over a cross-beam of the roof, like him on the sadler's horse in Fleet-street, upright: and he will sleep there.

CLER: But where are your collegiates?

DAUP: Withdrawn with the bride in private.

TRUE: O, they are instructing her in the college-grammar. If she have grace with them, she knows all their secrets instantly.

CLER: Methinks the lady Haughty looks well to-day, for all my dispraise of her in the morning. I think, I shall come about to thee again, Truewit.

TRUE: Believe it, I told you right. Women ought to repair the losses time and years have made in their features, with dressings. And an intelligent woman, if she know by herself the least defect, will be most curious to hide it: and it becomes her. If she be short, let her sit much, lest, when she stands, she be thought to sit. If she have an ill foot, let her wear her gown the longer, and her shoe the thinner. If a fat hand, and scald nails, let her carve the less, and act in gloves. If a sour breath, let her never discourse fasting, and always talk at her distance. If she have black and rugged teeth, let her offer the less at laughter, especially if she laugh wide and open.

CLER: O, you shall have some women, when they laugh, you would think they brayed, it is so rude, and—

TRUE: Ay, and others, that will stalk in their gait like an estrich, and take huge strides. I cannot endure such a sight. I love measure in the feet, and number in the voice: they are gentlenesses, that oftentimes draw no less than the face.

DAUP: How camest thou to study these creatures so exactly? I would thou would'st make me a proficient.

TRUE: Yes, but you must leave to live in your chamber, then, a month together upon Amadis de Gaul, or Don Quixote, as you are wont; and come abroad where the matter is frequent, to court, to tiltings, public shows and feasts, to plays, and church sometimes: thither they come to shew their new tires too, to see, and to be seen. In these places a man shall find whom to love, whom to play with, whom to touch once, whom to hold ever. The variety arrests his judgment. A wench to please a man comes not down dropping from the ceiling, as he lies on his back droning a tobacco pipe. He must go where she is.

DAUP: Yes, and be never the nearer.

TRUE: Out, heretic! That diffidence makes thee worthy it should be so.

CLER: He says true to you, Dauphine.

DAUP: Why?

TRUE: A man should not doubt to overcome any woman. Think he can vanquish them, and he shall: for though they deny, their desire is to be tempted. Penelope herself cannot hold out long. Ostend, you saw, was taken at last. You must persever, and hold to your purpose. They would solicit us, but that they are afraid. Howsoever, they wish in their hearts we should solicit them. Praise them, flatter them, you shall never want eloquence or trust: even the chastest delight to feel themselves that way rubb'd. With praises you must mix kisses too: if they take them, they'll take more—though they strive, they would be overcome.

CLER: O, but a man must beware of force.

TRUE: It is to them an acceptable violence, and has oft-times the place of the greatest courtesy. She that might have been forced, and you let her go free without touching, though then she seem to thank you, will ever hate you after; and glad in the face, is assuredly sad at the heart.

CLER: But all women are not to be taken all ways.

TRUE: 'Tis true; no more than all birds, or all fishes. If you appear learned to an ignorant wench, or jocund to a sad, or witty to a foolish, why she presently begins to mistrust herself. You must approach them in their own height, their own line: for the contrary makes many, that fear to commit themselves to noble and worthy fellows, run into the embraces of a rascal. If she love wit, give verses, though you borrow them of a friend, or buy them, to have good. If valour, talk of your sword, and be frequent in the mention of quarrels, though you be staunch in fighting. If activity, be seen on your barbary often, or leaping over stools, for the credit of your back. If she love good clothes or dressing, have your learned council about you every morning, your French tailor, barber, linener, etc. Let your powder, your glass, and your comb be your dearest acquaintance. Take more care for the

63

ornament of your head, than the safety: and wish the commonwealth rather troubled, than a hair about you. That will take her. Then, if she be covetous and craving, do you promise any thing, and perform sparingly; so shall you keep her in appetite still. Seem as you would give, but be like a barren field, that yields little, or unlucky dice to foolish and hoping gamesters. Let your gifts be slight and dainty, rather than precious. Let cunning be above cost. Give cherries at time of year, or apricots; and say they were sent you out of the country, though you bought them in Cheapside. Admire her tires: like her in all fashions; compare her in every habit to some deity; invent excellent dreams to flatter her, and riddles; or, if she be a great one, perform always the second parts to her: like what she likes, praise whom she praises, and fail not to make the household and servants yours, yea the whole family, and salute them by their names: ('tis but light cost if you can purchase them so,) and make her physician your pensioner, and her chief woman. Nor will it be out of your gain to make love to her too, so she follow, not usher her lady's pleasure. All blabbing is taken away, when she comes to be a part of the crime.

DAUP: On what courtly lap hast thou late slept, to come forth so sudden and absolute a courtling?

TRUE: Good faith, I should rather question you, that are so harkening after these mysteries. I begin to suspect your diligence, Dauphine. Speak, art thou in love in earnest?

DAUP: Yes, by my troth am I: 'twere ill dissembling before thee.

TRUE: With which of them, I prithee?

DAUP: With all the collegiates.

CLER: Out on thee! We'll keep you at home, believe it, in the stable, if you be such a stallion.

TRUE: No; I like him well. Men should love wisely, and all women; some one for the face, and let her please the eye; another for the skin, and let her please the touch; a third for the voice, and let her please the ear; and where the objects mix, let the senses so too. Thou would'st think it strange, if I should make them all in love with thee afore night!

DAUP: I would say, thou had'st the best philtre in the world, and couldst do more than madam Medea, or doctor Foreman.

TRUE: If I do not, let me play the mountebank for my meat, while I live, and the bawd for my drink.

DAUP: So be it, I say.

[ENTER OTTER, WITH HIS THREE CUPS, DAW, AND LA-FOOLE.]

OTT: O Lord, gentlemen, how my knights and I have mist you here!

CLER: Why, captain, what service? what service?

OTT: To see me bring up my bull, bear, and horse to fight.

DAW: Yes, faith, the captain says we shall be his dogs to bait them.

DAUP: A good employment.

TRUE: Come on, let's see a course, then.

LA-F: I am afraid my cousin will be offended, if she come.

OTT: Be afraid of nothing. Gentlemen, I have placed the drum and the trumpets, and one to give them the sign when you are ready. Here's my bull for myself, and my bear for sir John Daw, and my horse for sir Amorous. Now set your foot to mine, and yours to his, and—

LA-F: Pray God my cousin come not.

OTT: Saint George, and saint Andrew, fear no cousins. Come, sound, sound.
[DRUM AND TRUMPETS SOUND.]
Et rauco strepuerunt cornua cantu.

[THEY DRINK.]

TRUE: Well said, captain, i'faith: well fought at the bull.

CLER: Well held at the bear.

TRUE: Low, low! captain.

DAUP: O, the horse has kick'd off his dog already.

LA-F: I cannot drink it, as I am a knight.

TRUE: Ods so! off with his spurs, somebody.

LA-F: It goes against my conscience. My cousin will be angry with it.

DAW: I have done mine.

TRUE: You fought high and fair, sir John.

CLER: At the head.

DAUP: Like an excellent bear-dog.

CLER: You take no notice of the business, I hope?

DAW: Not a word, sir; you see we are jovial.

OTT: Sir Amorous, you must not equivocate.
It must be pull'd down, for all my cousin.

CLER: 'Sfoot, if you take not your drink, they will think you are discontented with something: you'll betray all, if you take the least notice.

LA-F: Not I; I'll both drink and talk then.

OTT: You must pull the horse on his knees, sir Amorous: fear no cousins. Jacta est alea.

TRUE: O, now he's in his vein, and bold. The least hint given him of his wife now, will make him rail desperately.

CLER: Speak to him of her.

TRUE: Do you, and I will fetch her to the hearing of it.

[EXIT.]

DAUP: Captain He-Otter, your She-Otter is coming, your wife.

OTT: Wife! buz! titivilitium! There's no such thing in nature.
I confess, gentlemen, I have a cook, a laundress, a house-drudge,
that serves my necessary turns, and goes under that title: but
he's an ass that will be so uxorious to tie his affections to one
circle. Come, the name dulls appetite. Here, replenish again:
another bout.
[FILLS THE CUPS AGAIN.]
Wives are nasty sluttish animalls.

DAUP: O, captain.

OTT: As ever the earth bare, tribus verbis. Where's master
Truewit?

DAW: He's slipt aside, sir.

CLER: But you must drink, and be jovial.

DAW: Yes, give it me.

LA-F: And me too.

DAW: Let's be jovial.

LA-F: As jovial as you will.

OTT: Agreed. Now you shall have the bear, cousin, and sir John
Daw the horse, and I will have the bull still. Sound, Tritons of
the Thames.
[DRUM AND TRUMPETS SOUND AGAIN.]
Nunc est bibendum, nunc pede libero—

MOR [ABOVE]: Villains, murderers, sons of the earth, and
traitors, what do you there?

CLER: O, now the trumpets have waked him, we shall have his
company.

OTT: A wife is a scurvy clogdogdo, an unlucky thing, a very

foresaid bear-whelp, without any good fashion or breeding: mala bestia.

[RE-ENTER TRUEWIT BEHIND, WITH MISTRESS OTTER.]

DAUP: Why did you marry one then, captain?

OTT: A pox!—I married with six thousand pound, I. I was in love with that. I have not kissed my Fury these forty weeks.

CLER: The more to blame you, captain.

TRUE: Nay, mistress Otter, hear him a little first.

OTT: She has a breath worse than my grandmother's, profecto.

MRS. OTT: O treacherous liar! kiss me, sweet master Truewit, and prove him a slandering knave.

TRUE: I will rather believe you, lady.

OTT: And she has a peruke that's like a pound of hemp, made up in shoe-threads.

MRS. OTT: O viper, mandrake!

OTT: A most vile face! and yet she spends me forty pound a year in mercury and hogs-bones. All her teeth were made in the Black-Friars, both her eyebrows in the Strand, and her hair in Silver-street. Every part of the town owns a piece of her.

MRS. OTT [COMES FORWARD.]: I cannot hold.

OTT: She takes herself asunder still when she goes to bed, into some twenty boxes; and about next day noon is put together again, like a great German clock: and so comes forth, and rings a tedious larum to the whole house, and then is quiet again for an hour, but for her quarters. Have you done me right, gentlemen?

MRS. OTT [FALLS UPON HIM, AND BEATS HIM.]: No, sir, I will do you right with my quarters, with my quarters.

OTT: O, hold, good princess.

TRUE: Sound, sound!

[DRUM AND TRUMPETS SOUND.]

CLER: A battle, a battle!

MRS. OTT: You notorious stinkardly bearward, does my breath smell?

OTT: Under correction, dear princess: look to my bear, and my horse, gentlemen.

MRS. OTT: Do I want teeth, and eyebrows, thou bull-dog?

TRUE: Sound, sound still.

[THEY SOUND AGAIN.]

OTT: No, I protest, under correction—

MRS. OTT: Ay, now you are under correction, you protest: but you did not protest before correction, sir. Thou Judas, to offer to betray thy princess! I will make thee an example—
[BEATS HIM.]

[ENTER MOROSE WITH HIS LONG SWORD.]

MOR: I will have no such examples in my house, lady Otter.

MRS. OTT: Ah!—

[MRS. OTTER, DAW, AND LA-FOOLE RUN OFF.]

OTT: Mistress Mary Ambree, your examples are dangerous. Rogues, hell-hounds, Stentors! out of my doors, you sons of noise and tumult, begot on an ill May-day, or when the galley-foist is afloat to Westminster!
[DRIVES OUT THE MUSICIANS.]
A trumpeter could not be conceived but then!

DAUP: What ails you, sir?

MOR: They have rent my roof, walls, and all my windows asunder, with their brazen throats.

69

[EXIT.]

TRUE: Best follow him, Dauphine.

DAUP: So I will.
[EXIT.]

CLER: Where's Daw and La-Foole?

OTT: They are both run away, sir. Good gentlemen, help to pacify my princess, and speak to the great ladies for me. Now must I go lie with the bears this fortnight, and keep out of the way, till my peace be made, for this scandal she has taken. Did you not see my bull-head, gentlemen?

CLER: Is't not on, captain?

TRUE: No; but he may make a new one, by that is on.

OTT: O, here it is. An you come over, gentlemen, and ask for Tom Otter, we'll go down to Ratcliff, and have a course i'faith, for all these disasters. There is bona spes left.

TRUE: Away, captain, get off while you are well.

[EXIT OTTER.]

CLER: I am glad we are rid of him.

TRUE: You had never been, unless we had put his wife upon him. His humour is as tedious at last, as it was ridiculous at first.

[EXEUNT.]

SCENE 4.2.

A LONG OPEN GALLERY IN THE SAME.

ENTER LADY HAUGHTY, MISTRESS OTTER, MAVIS, DAW, LAFOOLE, CENTAURE, AND EPICOENE.

HAU: We wonder'd why you shriek'd so, mistress Otter?

MRS. OTT: O lord, madam, he came down with a huge long naked weapon in both his hands, and look'd so dreadfully! sure he's beside himself.

HAU: Why, what made you there, mistress Otter?

MRS. OTT: Alas, mistress Mavis, I was chastising my subject, and thought nothing of him.

DAW: Faith, mistress, you must do so too: learn to chastise. Mistress Otter corrects her husband so, he dares not speak but under correction.

LA-F: And with his hat off to her: 'twould do you good to see.

HAU: In sadness, 'tis good and mature counsel: practise it, Morose. I'll call you Morose still now, as I call Centaure and Mavis; we four will be all one.

CEN: And you will come to the college, and live with us?

HAU: Make him give milk and honey.

MAV: Look how you manage him at first, you shall have him ever after.

CEN: Let him allow you your coach, and four horses, your woman, your chamber-maid, your page, your gentleman-usher, your French cook, and four grooms.

HAU: And go with us to Bedlam, to the china-houses, and to the Exchange.

71

CEN: It will open the gate to your fame.

HAU: Here's Centaure has immortalised herself, with taming of her wild male.

MAV: Ay, she has done the miracle of the kingdom.

[ENTER CLERIMONT AND TRUEWIT.]

EPI: But, ladies, do you count it lawful to have such plurality of servants, and do them all graces?

HAU: Why not? why should women deny their favours to men? are they the poorer or the worse?

DAW: Is the Thames the less for the dyer's water, mistress?

LA-F: Or a torch for lighting many torches?

TRUE: Well said, La-Foole; what a new one he has got!

CEN: They are empty losses women fear in this kind.

HAU: Besides, ladies should be mindful of the approach of age, and let no time want his due use. The best of our days pass first.

MAV: We are rivers, that cannot be call'd back, madam: she that now excludes her lovers, may live to lie a forsaken beldame, in a frozen bed.

CEN: 'Tis true, Mavis: and who will wait on us to coach then? or write, or tell us the news then, make anagrams of our names, and invite us to the Cockpit, and kiss our hands all the play-time, and draw their weapons for our honours?

HAU: Not one.

DAW: Nay, my mistress is not altogether unintelligent of these things; here be in presence have tasted of her favours.

CLER: What a neighing hobby-horse is this!

EPI: But not with intent to boast them again, servant. And have

72

you those excellent receipts, madam, to keep yourselves from bearing of children?

HAU: O yes, Morose: how should we maintain our youth and beauty else? Many births of a woman make her old, as many crops make the earth barren.

[ENTER MOROSE AND DAUPHINE.]

MOR: O my cursed angel, that instructed me to this fate!

DAUP: Why, sir?

MOR: That I should be seduced by so foolish a devil as a barber will make!

DAUP: I would I had been worthy, sir, to have partaken your counsel; you should never have trusted it to such a minister.

MOR: Would I could redeem it with the loss of an eye, nephew, a hand, or any other member.

DAUP: Marry, God forbid, sir, that you should geld yourself, to anger your wife.

MOR: So it would rid me of her! and, that I did supererogatory penance in a belfry, at Westminster-hall, in the Cock-pit, at the fall of a stag; the Tower-wharf (what place is there else?)— London-bridge, Paris-garden, Billinsgate, when the noises are at their height, and loudest. Nay, I would sit out a play, that were nothing but fights at sea, drum, trumpet, and target.

DAUP: I hope there shall be no such need, sir. Take patience, good uncle. This is but a day, and 'tis well worn too now.

MOR: O, 'twill be so for ever, nephew, I foresee it, for ever. Strife and tumult are the dowry that comes with a wife.

TRUE: I told you so, sir, and you would not believe me.

MOR: Alas, do not rub those wounds, master Truewit, to blood again: 'twas my negligence. Add not affliction to affliction. I have perceived the effect of it, too late, in madam Otter.

EPI: How do you, sir?

MOR: Did you ever hear a more unnecessary question? as if she did not see! Why, I do as you see, empress, empress.

EPI: You are not well, sir; you look very ill; something has distemper'd you.

MOR: O horrible, monstrous impertinencies! would not one of these have served, do you think, sir? would not one of these have served?

TRUE: Yes, sir, but these are but notes of female kindness, sir; certain tokens that she has a voice, sir.

MOR: O, is it so? Come, an't be no otherwise—What say you?

EPI: How do you feel yourself, sir?

MOR: Again that!

TRUE: Nay, look you, sir: you would be friends with your wife upon unconscionable terms; her silence—

EPI: They say you are run mad, sir.

MOR: Not for love, I assure you, of you; do you see?

EPI: O lord, gentlemen! lay hold on him, for God's sake. What shall I do? who's his physician, can you tell, that knows the state of his body best, that I might send for him? Good sir, speak; I'll send for one of my doctors else.

MOR: What, to poison me, that I might die intestate, and leave you possest of all?

EPI: Lord, how idly he talks, and how his eyes sparkle! he looks green about the temples! do you see what blue spots he has?

TRUE: Ay, 'tis melancholy.

EPI: Gentlemen, for Heaven's sake, counsel me. Ladies;—servant, you have read Pliny and Paracelsus; ne'er a word now to comfort a poor gentlewoman? Ay me, what fortune had I, to marry a distracted man!

DAW: I will tell you, mistress—

TRUE: How rarely she holds it up!
[ASIDE TO CLER.]

MOR: What mean you, gentlemen?

EPI: What will you tell me, servant?

DAW: The disease in Greek is called mania, in Latin insania, furor, vel ecstasis melancholica, that is, egressio, when a man ex melancholico evadit fanaticus.

MOR: Shall I have a lecture read upon me alive?

DAW: But he may be but phreneticus yet, mistress? and phrenetis is only delirium, or so.

EPI: Ay, that is for the disease, servant: but what is this to the cure? we are sure enough of the disease.

MOR: Let me go.

TRUE: Why, we'll entreat her to hold her peace, sir.

MOR: O no, labour not to stop her. She is like a conduit-pipe, that will gush out with more force when she opens again.

HAU: I will tell you, Morose, you must talk divinity to him altogether, or moral philosophy.

LA-F: Ay, and there's an excellent book of moral philosophy, madam, of Raynard the fox, and all the beasts, called Doni's Philosophy.

CEN: There is, indeed, sir Amorous La-Foole.

MOR: O misery!

LA-F: I have read it, my lady Centaure, all over, to my cousin, here.

75

MRS. OTT: Ay, and 'tis a very good book as any is, of the moderns.

DAW: Tut, he must have Seneca read to him, and Plutarch, and the ancients; the moderns are not for this disease.

CLER: Why, you discommended them too, to-day, sir John.

DAW: Ay, in some cases: but in these they are best, and Aristotle's ethics.

MAV: Say you so sir John? I think you are decived: you took it upon trust.

HAU: Where's Trusty, my woman? I'll end this difference. I prithee, Otter, call her. Her father and mother were both mad, when they put her to me.

MOR: I think so. Nay, gentlemen, I am tame. This is but an exercise, I know, a marriage ceremony, which I must endure.

HAU: And one of them, I know not which, was cur'd with the Sick Man's Salve; and the other with Green's Groat's-worth of Wit.

TRUE: A very cheap cure, madam.

[ENTER TRUSTY.]

HAU: Ay, 'tis very feasible.

MRS. OTT: My lady call'd for you, mistress Trusty: you must decide a controversy.

HAU: O, Trusty, which was it you said, your father, or your mother, that was cured with the Sick Man's Salve?

TRUS: My mother, madam, with the Salve.

TRUE: Then it was the sick woman's salve?

TRUS: And my father with the Groat's-worth of Wit. But there was other means used: we had a preacher that would preach folk asleep still; and so they were prescribed to go to church, by an old woman that was their physician, thrice a week—

EPI: To sleep?

TRUS: Yes, forsooth: and every night they read themselves asleep on those books.

EPI: Good faith, it stands with great reason. I would I knew where to procure those books.

MOR: Oh!

LA-F: I can help you with one of them, mistress Morose, the Groat's-worth of Wit.

EPI: But I shall disfurnish you, sir Amorous: can you spare it?

LA-F: O, yes, for a week, or so; I'll read it myself to him.

EPI: No, I must do that, sir: that must be my office.

MOR: Oh, oh!

EPI: Sure he would do well enough, if he could sleep.

MOR: No, I should do well enough, if you could sleep. Have I no friend that will make her drunk? or give her a little laudanum? or opium?

TRUE: Why, sir, she talks ten times worse in her sleep.

MOR: How!

CLER: Do you not know that, sir? never ceases all night.

TRUE: And snores like a porpoise.

MOR: O, redeem me, fate; redeem me, fate! For how many causes may a man be divorced, nephew?

DAUP: I know not, truly, sir.

TRUE: Some divine must resolve you in that, sir, or canon-lawyer.

MOR: I will not rest, I will not think of any other hope or comfort, till I know.

[EXIT WITH DAUPHINE.]

CLER: Alas, poor man!

TRUE: You'll make him mad indeed, ladies, if you pursue this.

HAU: No, we'll let him breathe now, a quarter of an hour or so.

CLER: By my faith, a large truce!

HAU: Is that his keeper, that is gone with him?

DAW: It is his nephew, madam.

LA-F: Sir Dauphine Eugenie.

HAU: He looks like a very pitiful knight—

DAW: As can be. This marriage has put him out of all.

LA-F: He has not a penny in his purse, madam.

DAW: He is ready to cry all this day.

LA-F: A very shark; he set me in the nick t'other night at Primero.

TRUE: How these swabbers talk!

CLER: Ay, Otter's wine has swell'd their humours above a spring-tide.

HAU: Good Morose, let us go in again. I like your couches exceeding well; we will go lie and talk there.

[EXEUNT HAU., CEN., MAV., TRUS., LA-FOOLE, AND DAW.]

EPI [FOLLOWING THEM.]: I wait on you, madam.

TRUE [STOPPING HER.]: 'Slight, I will have them as silent as signs, and their post too, ere I have done. Do you hear, lady-bride? I pray thee now, as thou art a noble wench, continue this discourse of Dauphine within; but praise him exceedingly: magnify him with all the height of affection thou canst;—I have some purpose in't:

78

and but beat off these two rooks, Jack Daw and his fellow, with any discontentment, hither, and I'll honour thee for ever.

EPI: I was about it here. It angered me to the soul, to hear them begin to talk so malepert.

TRUE: Pray thee perform it, and thou winn'st me an idolater to thee everlasting.

EPI: Will you go in and hear me do't?

TRUE: No, I'll stay here. Drive them out of your company, 'tis all I ask; which cannot be any way better done, than by extolling Dauphine, whom they have so slighted.

EPI: I warrant you; you shall expect one of them presently.

[EXIT.]

CLER: What a cast of kestrils are these, to hawk after ladies, thus!

TRUE: Ay, and strike at such an eagle as Dauphine.

CLER: He will be mad when we tell him. Here he comes.

[RE-ENTER DAUPHINE.]

CLER: O sir, you are welcome.

TRUE: Where's thine uncle?

DAUP: Run out of doors in his night-caps, to talk with a casuist about his divorce. It works admirably.

TRUE: Thou wouldst have said so, if thou hadst been here! The ladies have laugh'd at thee most comically, since thou went'st, Dauphine.

CLER: And ask'd, if thou wert thine uncle's keeper.

TRUE: And the brace of baboons answer'd, Yes; and said thou wert a pitiful poor fellow, and didst live upon posts: and hadst nothing but three suits of apparel, and some few benevolences that lords gave thee to fool to them, and swagger.

DAUP: Let me not live, I will beat them: I'll bind them both to grand-madam's bed-posts, and have them baited with monkies.

TRUE: Thou shalt not need, they shall be beaten to thy hand, Dauphine. I have an execution to serve upon them, I warrant thee, shall serve; trust my plot.

DAUP: Ay, you have many plots! so you had one to make all the wenches in love with me.

TRUE: Why, if I do not yet afore night, as near as 'tis; and that they do not every one invite thee, and be ready to scratch for thee, take the mortgage of my wit.

CLER: 'Fore God, I'll be his witness thou shalt have it, Dauphine: thou shalt be his fool for ever, if thou doest not.

TRUE: Agreed. Perhaps 'twill be the better estate. Do you observe this gallery, or rather lobby, indeed? Here are a couple of studies, at each end one: here will I act such a tragi-comedy between the Guelphs and the Ghibellines, Daw and La-Foole— which of them comes out first, will I seize on:—you two shall be the chorus behind the arras, and whip out between the acts and speak—If I do not make them keep the peace for this remnant of the day, if not of the year, I have failed once—I hear Daw coming: hide, [THEY WITHDRAW] and do not laugh, for God's sake.

[RE-ENTER DAW.]

DAW: Which is the way into the garden trow?

TRUE: O, Jack Daw! I am glad I have met with you. In good faith, I must have this matter go no further between you. I must have it taken up.

DAW: What matter, sir? between whom?

TRUE: Come, you disguise it: sir Amorous and you. If you love me, Jack, you shall make use of your philosophy now, for this once, and deliver me your sword. This is not the wedding the Centaurs were at, though there be a she one here.

80

[TAKES HIS SWORD.]
The bride has entreated me I will see no blood shed at her bridal,
you saw her whisper me erewhile.

DAW: As I hope to finish Tacitus, I intend no murder.

TRUE: Do you not wait for sir Amorous?

DAW: Not I, by my knighthood.

TRUE: And your scholarship too?

DAW: And my scholarship too.

TRUE: Go to, then I return you your sword, and ask you mercy;
but put it not up, for you will be assaulted. I understood that you
had apprehended it, and walked here to brave him: and that you
had held your life contemptible, in regard of your honour.

DAW: No, no; no such thing, I assure you. He and I parted now,
as good friends as could be.

TRUE: Trust not you to that visor. I saw him since dinner with
another face: I have known many men in my time vex'd with
losses, with deaths, and with abuses; but so offended a wight as sir
Amorous, did I never see, or read of. For taking away his guests,
sir, to-day, that's the cause: and he declares it behind your back
with such threatenings and contempts—He said to Dauphine, you
were the arrant'st ass—

DAW: Ay, he may say his pleasure.

TRUE: And swears you are so protested a coward, that he knows
you will never do him any manly or single right, and therefore he
will take his course.

DAW: I'll give him any satisfaction, sir—but fighting.

TRUE: Ay, sir: but who knows what satisfaction he'll take? blood
he thirsts for, and blood he will have: and whereabouts on you he
will have it, who knows but himself?

DAW: I pray you, master Truewit, be you a mediator.

TRUE: Well, sir, conceal yourself then in this study till I
return.
[PUTS HIM INTO THE STUDY.]
Nay, you must be content to be lock'd in: for, for mine own
reputation, I would not have you seen to receive a public
disgrace, while I have the matter in managing. Ods so, here he
comes; keep your breath close, that he do not hear you sigh.
In good faith, sir Amorous, he is not this way; I pray you be
merciful, do not murder him; he is a Christian, as good as you:
you are arm'd as if you sought revenge on all his race. Good
Dauphine, get him away from this place. I never knew a man's
choler so high, but he would speak to his friends, he would hear
reason.—Jack Daw, Jack! asleep!

DAW [within]: Is he gone, master Truewit?

TRUE: Ay; did you hear him?

DAW: O lord! yes.

TRUE: What a quick ear fear has!

DAW [COMES OUT OF THE CLOSET.]: But is he so arm'd, as you
say?

TRUE: Arm'd? did you ever see a fellow set out to take possession?

DAW: Ay, sir.

TRUE: That may give you some light to conceive of him: but 'tis
nothing to the principal. Some false brother in the house has
furnish'd him strangely; or, if it were out of the house, it was
Tom Otter.

DAW: Indeed he's a captain, and his wife is his kinswoman.

TRUE: He has got some body's old two-hand sword, to mow you
off at the knees; and that sword hath spawn'd such a dagger!—But
then he is so hung with pikes, halberds, petronels, calivers and
muskets, that he looks like a justice of peace's hall: a man of
two thousand a-year, is not cess'd at so many weapons as he has
on. There was never fencer challenged at so many several foils.
You would think he meant to murder all Saint Pulchre parish. If he

could but victual himself for half a year in his breeches, he is sufficiently arm'd to over-run a country.

DAW: Good lord! what means he, sir? I pray you, master Truewit, be you a mediator.

TRUE: Well, I 'll try if he will be appeased with a leg or an arm; if not you must die once.

DAW: I would be loth to lose my right arm, for writing madrigals.

TRUE: Why, if he will be satisfied with a thumb or a little finger, all's one to me. You must think, I will do my best.

[SHUTS HIM UP AGAIN.]

DAW: Good sir, do.

[CLERIMONT AND DAUPHINE COME FORWARD.]

CLER: What hast thou done?

TRUE: He will let me do nothing, he does all afore; he offers his left arm.

CLER: His left wing for a Jack Daw.

DAUP: Take it, by all means.

TRUE: How! maim a man for ever, for a jest? What a conscience hast thou!

DAUP: 'Tis no loss to him; he has no employment for his arms, but to eat spoon-meat. Beside, as good maim his body as his reputation.

TRUE: He is a scholar, and a wit, and yet he does not think so. But he loses no reputation with us; for we all resolved him an ass before. To your places again.

CLER: I pray thee, let me be in at the other a little.

TRUE: Look, you'll spoil all: these be ever your tricks.

83

CLER: No, but I could hit of some things that thou wilt miss, and thou wilt say are good ones.

TRUE: I warrant you. I pray forbear, I will leave it off, else.

DAUP: Come away, Clerimont.

[DAUP. AND CLER. WITHDRAW AS BEFORE.]

[ENTER LA-FOOLE.]

TRUE: Sir Amorous!

LA-F: Master Truewit.

TRUE: Whither were you going?

LA-F: Down into the court to make water.

TRUE: By no means, sir; you shall rather tempt your breeches.

LA-F: Why, sir?

TRUE: Enter here, if you love your life.

[OPENING THE DOOR OF THE OTHER STUDY.]

LA-F: Why? why?

TRUE: Question till you throat be cut, do: dally till the enraged soul find you.

LA-F: Who is that?

TRUE: Daw it is: will you in?

LA-F: Ay, ay, I will in: what's the matter?

TRUE: Nay, if he had been cool enough to tell us that, there had been some hope to atone you, but he seems so implacably enraged!

LA-F: 'Slight, let him rage! I'll hide myself.

TRUE: Do, good sir. But what have you done to him within, that should provoke him thus? You have broke some jest upon him, afore the ladies.

LA-F: Not I, never in my life, broke jest upon any man. The bride was praising sir Dauphine, and he went away in snuff, and I followed him, unless he took offence at me in his drink erewhile, that I would not pledge all the horse full.

TRUE: By my faith, and that may be, you remember well: but he walks the round up and down, through every room o' the house, with a towel in his hand, crying, Where's La-Foole? Who saw La-Foole? and when Dauphine and I demanded the cause, we can force no answer from him, but—O revenge, how sweet art thou! I will strangle him in this towel—which leads us to conjecture that the main cause of his fury is, for bringing your meat to-day, with a towel about you, to his discredit.

LA-F: Like enough. Why, if he be angry for that, I'll stay here till his anger be blown over.

TRUE: A good becoming resolution, sir; if you can put it on o' the sudden.

LA-F: Yes, I can put it on: or, I'll away into the country presently.

TRUE: How will you get out of the house, sir? he knows you are in the house, and he will watch you this se'ennight, but he'll have you. He'll outwait a serjeant for you.

LA-F: Why, then I'll stay here.

TRUE: You must think how to victual yourself in time then.

LA-F: Why, sweet master Truewit, will you entreat my cousin Otter to send me a cold venison pasty, a bottle or two of wine, and a chamber-pot?

TRUE: A stool were better, sir, of sir Ajax his invention.

LA-F: Ay, that will be better, indeed; and a pallet to lie on.

TRUE: O, I would not advise you to sleep by any means.

85

LA-F: Would you not, sir? why, then I will not.

TRUE: Yet, there's another fear—

LA-F: Is there! what is't?

TRUE: No, he cannot break open this door with his foot, sure.

LA-F: I'll set my back against it, sir. I have a good back.

TRUE: But then if he should batter.

LA-F: Batter! if he dare, I'll have an action of battery against him.

TRUE: Cast you the worst. He has sent for powder already, and what he will do with it, no man knows: perhaps blow up the corner of the house where he suspects you are. Here he comes; in quickly.
[THRUSTS IN LA-FOOLE AND SHUTS THE DOOR.]
I protest, sir John Daw, he is not this way: what will you do? before God, you shall hang no petard here. I'll die rather. Will you not take my word? I never knew one but would be satisfied.—
Sir Amorous,
[SPEAKS THROUGH THE KEY-HOLE,]
there's no standing out: He has made a petard of an old brass pot, to force your door. Think upon some satisfaction, or terms to offer him.

LA-F [WITHIN.]: Sir, I will give him any satisfaction: I dare give any terms.

TRUE: You'll leave it to me, then?

LA-F: Ay, sir. I'll stand to any conditions.

TRUE [BECKONING FORWARD CLERIMONT AND DAUPHINE.]: How now, what think you, sirs? were't not a difficult thing to determine which of these two fear'd most.

CLER: Yes, but this fears the bravest: the other a whiniling dastard, Jack Daw! But La-Foole, a brave heroic coward! and is afraid in a great look and a stout accent; I like him rarely.

86

TRUE: Had it not been pity these two should have been concealed?

CLER: Shall I make a motion?

TRUE: Briefly: For I must strike while 'tis hot.

CLER: Shall I go fetch the ladies to the catastrophe?

TRUE: Umph! ay, by my troth.

DAUP: By no mortal means. Let them continue in the state of ignorance, and err still; think them wits and fine fellows, as they have done. 'Twere sin to reform them.

TRUE: Well, I will have them fetch'd, now I think on't, for a private purpose of mine: do, Clerimont, fetch them, and discourse to them all that's past, and bring them into the gallery here.

DAUP: This is thy extreme vanity, now: thou think'st thou wert undone, if every jest thou mak'st were not publish'd.

TRUE: Thou shalt see how unjust thou art presently. Clerimont, say it was Dauphine's plot.
[EXIT CLERIMONT.]
Trust me not, if the whole drift be not for thy good. There is a carpet in the next room, put it on, with this scarf over thy face, and a cushion on thy head, and be ready when I call Amorous. Away!
[EXIT DAUP.]
John Daw!
[GOES TO DAW'S CLOSET AND BRINGS HIM OUT.]

DAW: What good news, sir?

TRUE: Faith, I have followed and argued with him hard for you. I told him you were a knight, and a scholar, and that you knew fortitude did consist magis patiendo quam faciendo, magis ferendo quam feriendo.

DAW: It doth so indeed, sir.

TRUE: And that you would suffer, I told him: so at first he demanded by my troth, in my conceit, too much.

87

DAW: What was it, sir.

TRUE: Your upper lip, and six of your fore-teeth.

DAW: 'Twas unreasonable.

TRUE: Nay, I told him plainly, you could not spare them all.
So after long argument pro et con as you know, I brought him
down to your two butter-teeth, and them he would have.

DAW: O, did you so? Why, he shall have them.

TRUE: But he shall not, sir, by your leave. The conclusion is this,
sir: because you shall be very good friends hereafter, and this
never to be remembered or upbraided; besides, that he may not
boast he has done any such thing to you in his own person: he is
to come here in disguise, give you five kicks in private, sir, take
your sword from you, and lock you up in that study during
pleasure: which will be but a little while, we'll get it released
presently.

DAW: Five kicks! he shall have six, sir, to be friends.

TRUE: Believe me, you shall not over-shoot yourself, to send him
that word by me.

DAW: Deliver it, sir: he shall have it with all my heart, to be
friends.

TRUE: Friends! Nay, an he should not be so, and heartily too,
upon these terms, he shall have me to enemy while I live. Come,
sir, bear it bravely.

DAW: O lord, sir, 'tis nothing.

TRUE: True: what's six kicks to a man that reads Seneca?

DAW: I have had a hundred, sir.

TRUE: Sir Amorous!
[RE-ENTER DAUPHINE, DISGUISED.]
No speaking one to another, or rehearsing old matters.

DAW [AS DAUPHINE KICKS HIM.]: One, two, three, four, five. I
protest, sir Amorous, you shall have six.

88

TRUE: Nay, I told you, you should not talk. Come give him six, an he will needs.
[DAUPHINE KICKS HIM AGAIN.]
—Your sword.
[TAKES HIS SWORD.]
Now return to your safe custody: you shall presently meet afore the ladies, and be the dearest friends one to another.
[PUTS DAW INTO THE STUDY.]
—Give me the scarf now, thou shalt beat the other bare-faced. Stand by:
[DAUPHINE RETIRES, AND TRUEWIT GOES TO THE OTHER CLOSET, AND
RELEASES LA-FOOLE.]
—Sir Amorous!

LA-F: What's here? A sword?

TRUE: I cannot help it, without I should take the quarrel upon myself. Here he has sent you his sword—

LA-F: I will receive none on't.

TRUE: And he wills you to fasten it against a wall, and break your head in some few several places against the hilts.

LA-F: I will not: tell him roundly. I cannot endure to shed my own blood.

TRUE: Will you not?

LA-F: No. I'll beat it against a fair flat wall, if that will satisfy him: if not, he shall beat it himself, for Amorous.

TRUE: Why, this is strange starting off, when a man undertakes for you! I offer'd him another condition; will you stand to that?

LA-F: Ay, what is't.

TRUE: That you will be beaten in private.

LA-F: Yes, I am content, at the blunt.

[ENTER, ABOVE, HAUGHTY, CENTAURE, MAVIS, MISTRESS OTTER, EPICOENE, AND TRUSTY.]

TRUE: Then you must submit yourself to be hoodwinked in this scarf, and be led to him, where he will take your sword from you, and make you bear a blow over the mouth, gules, and tweaks by the nose, sans nombre.

LA-F: I am content. But why must I be blinded?

TRUE: That's for your good, sir: because, if he should grow insolent upon this, and publish it hereafter to your disgrace, (which I hope he will not do,) you might swear safely, and protest, he never beat you, to your knowledge.

LA-F: O, I conceive.

TRUE: I do not doubt but you will be perfect good friends upon't, and not dare to utter an ill thought one of another in future.

LA-F: Not I, as God help me, of him.

TRUE: Nor he of you, sir. If he should
[BLINDS HIS EYES.]
—Come, sir.
[LEADS HIM FORWARD.]
—All hid, sir John.

[ENTER DAUPHINE, AND TWEAKS HIM BY THE NOSE.]

LA-F: O, sir John, sir John! Oh, o—o—o—o—o—Oh—

TRUE: Good, sir John, leave tweaking, you'll blow his nose off.
'Tis sir John's pleasure, you should retire into the study.
[PUTS HIM UP AGAIN.]
—Why, now you are friends. All bitterness between you, I hope, is buried; you shall come forth by and by, Damon and Pythias upon't, and embrace with all the rankness of friendship that can be. I trust, we shall have them tamer in their language hereafter. Dauphine, I worship thee.—Gods will the ladies have surprised us!

[ENTER HAUGHTY, CENTAURE, MAVIS, MISTRESS OTTER, EPICOENE, AND TRUSTY, BEHIND.]

HAU: Centaure, how our judgments were imposed on by these adulterate knights! Nay, madam, Mavis was more deceived than we, 'twas her commendation utter'd them in the college.

90

MAV: I commended but their wits, madam, and their braveries. I never look'd toward their valours.

HAU: Sir Dauphine is valiant, and a wit too, it seems.

MAV: And a bravery too.

HAU: Was this his project?

MRS. OTT: So master Clerimont intimates, madam.

HAU: Good Morose, when you come to the college, will you bring him with you? he seems a very perfect gentleman.

EPI: He is so, madam, believe it.

CEN: But when will you come, Morose?

EPI: Three or four days hence, madam, when I have got me a coach and horses.

HAU: No, to-morrow, good Morose; Centaure shall send you her coach.

MAV: Yes faith, do, and bring sir Dauphine with you.

HAU: She has promised that, Mavis.

MAV: He is a very worthy gentleman in his exteriors, madam.

HAU: Ay, he shews he is judicial in his clothes.

CEN: And yet not so superlatively neat as some, madam, that have their faces set in a brake.

HAU: Ay, and have every hair in form!

MAV: That wear purer linen then ourselves, and profess more neatness than the French hermaphrodite!

EPI: Ay, ladies, they, what they tell one of us, have told a thousand; and are the only thieves of our fame: that think to take us with that perfume, or with that lace, and laugh at us unconscionably when they have done.

91

HAU: But, sir Dauphine's carelessness becomes him.

CEN: I could love a man for such a nose.

MAV: Or such a leg!

CEN: He has an exceeding good eye, madam.

MAV: And a very good lock.

CEN: Good Morose, bring him to my chamber first.

MRS. OTT: Please your honours to meet at my house, madam.

TRUE: See how they eye thee, man! they are taken, I warrant thee.

[HAUGHTY COMES FORWARD.]

HAU: You have unbraced our brace of knights here, master Truewit.

TRUE: Not I, madam; it was sir Dauphine's ingine: who, if he have disfurnish'd your ladyship of any guard or service by it, is able to make the place good again, in himself.

HAU: There is no suspicion of that, sir.

CEN: God so, Mavis, Haughty is kissing.

MAV: Let us go too, and take part.

[THEY COME FORWARD.]

HAU: But I am glad of the fortune (beside the discovery of two such empty caskets) to gain the knowledge of so rich a mine of virtue as sir Dauphine.

CEN: We would be all glad to style him of our friendship, and see him at the college.

MAV: He cannot mix with a sweeter society, I'll prophesy; and I hope he himself will think so.

DAUP: I should be rude to imagine otherwise, lady.

TRUE: Did not I tell thee, Dauphine? Why, all their actions are governed by crude opinion, without reason or cause; they know not why they do any thing: but, as they are inform'd, believe, judge, praise, condemn, love, hate, and in emulation one of another, do all these things alike. Only they have a natural inclination sways them generally to the worst, when they are left to themselves. But pursue it, now thou hast them.

HAU: Shall we go in again, Morose?

EPI: Yes, madam.

CEN: We'll entreat sir Dauphine's company.

TRUE: Stay, good madam, the interview of the two friends, Pylades and Orestes: I'll fetch them out to you straight.

HAU: Will you, master Truewit?

DAUP: Ay, but noble ladies, do not confess in your countenance, or outward bearing to them, any discovery of their follies, that we may see how they will bear up again, with what assurance and erection.

HAU: We will not, sir Dauphine.

CEN. MAV: Upon our honours, sir Dauphine.

TRUE [GOES TO THE FIRST CLOSET.]: Sir Amorous, sir Amorous! The ladies are here.

LA-F [WITHIN.]: Are they?

TRUE: Yes; but slip out by and by, as their backs are turn'd, and meet sir John here, as by chance, when I call you.
[goes to the other.]
—Jack Daw.

DAW: What say you, sir?

TRUE: Whip out behind me suddenly, and no anger in your looks to your adversary. Now, now!

[LA-FOOLE AND DAW SLIP OUT OF THEIR RESPECTIVE CLOSETS, AND SALUTE EACH OTHER.]

93

LA-F: Noble sir John Daw, where have you been?

DAW: To seek you, sir Amorous.

LA-F: Me! I honour you.

DAW: I prevent you, sir.

CLER: They have forgot their rapiers.

TRUE: O, they meet in peace, man.

DAUP: Where's your sword, sir John?

CLER: And yours, sir Amorous?

DAW: Mine! my boy had it forth to mend the handle, e'en now.

LA-F: And my gold handle was broke too, and my boy had it forth.

DAUP: Indeed, sir!—How their excuses meet!

CLER: What a consent there is in the handles!

TRUE: Nay, there is so in the points too, I warrant you.

[ENTER MOROSE, WITH THE TWO SWORDS, DRAWN IN HIS HANDS.]

MRS. OTT: O me! madam, he comes again, the madman! Away!

[LADIES, DAW, AND LA-FOOLE, RUN OFF.]

MOR: What make these naked weapons here, gentlemen?

TRUE: O sir! here hath like to have been murder since you went; a couple of knights fallen out about the bride's favours! We were fain to take away their weapons; your house had been begg'd by this time else.

MOR: For what?

CLER: For manslaughter, sir, as being accessary.

94

MOR: And for her favours?

TRUE: Ay, sir, heretofore, not present—Clerimont, carry them their swords, now. They have done all the hurt they will do.

[EXIT CLER. WITH THE TWO SWORDS.]

DAUP: Have you spoke with the lawyer, sir?

MOR: O, no! there is such a noise in the court, that they have frighted me home with more violence then I went! such speaking and counter-speaking, with their several voices of citations, appellations, allegations, certificates, attachments, intergatories, references, convictions, and afflictions indeed, among the doctors and proctors, that the noise here is silence to't! a kind of calm midnight!

TRUE: Why, sir, if you would be resolved indeed, I can bring you hither a very sufficient lawyer, and a learned divine, that shall enquire into every least scruple for you.

MOR: Can you, master Truewit?

TRUE: Yes, and are very sober, grave persons, that will dispatch it in a chamber, with a whisper or two.

MOR: Good sir, shall I hope this benefit from you, and trust myself into your hands?

TRUE: Alas, sir! your nephew and I have been ashamed and oft-times mad, since you went, to think how you are abused. Go in, good sir, and lock yourself up till we call you; we'll tell you more anon, sir.

MOR: Do your pleasure with me gentlemen; I believe in you: and that deserves no delusion.

[EXIT.]

TRUE: You shall find none, sir: but heap'd, heap'd plenty of vexation.

DAUP: What wilt thou do now, Wit?

TRUE: Recover me hither Otter and the barber, if you can, by any means, presently.

DAUP: Why? to what purpose?

TRUE: O, I'll make the deepest divine, and gravest lawyer, out of them two for him—

DAUP: Thou canst not, man; these are waking dreams.

TRUE: Do not fear me. Clap but a civil gown with a welt on the one; and a canonical cloak with sleeves on the other: and give them a few terms in their mouths, if there come not forth as able a doctor, and complete a parson, for this turn, as may be wish'd, trust not my election: and, I hope, without wronging the dignity of either profession, since they are but persons put on, and for mirth's sake, to torment him. The barber smatters Latin, I remember.

DAUP: Yes, and Otter too.

TRUE: Well then, if I make them not wrangle out this case to his no comfort, let me be thought a Jack Daw or La-Foole or anything worse. Go you to your ladies, but first send for them.

DAUP: I will.

[EXEUNT.]

ACT 5

SCENE 5.1.

A ROOM IN MOROSE'S HOUSE.

ENTER LA-FOOLE, CLERIMONT, AND DAW.

LA-F: Where had you our swords, master Clerimont?

CLER: Why, Dauphine took them from the madman.

LA-F: And he took them from our boys, I warrant you.

CLER: Very like, sir.

LA-F: Thank you, good master Clerimont. Sir John Daw and I are both beholden to you.

CLER: Would I knew how to make you so, gentlemen!

DAW: Sir Amorous and I are your servants, sir.

[ENTER MAVIS.]

MAV: Gentlemen, have any of you a pen and ink? I would fain write out a riddle in Italian, for sir Dauphine, to translate.

CLER: Not I, in troth lady; I am no scrivener.

DAW: I can furnish you, I think, lady.

[EXEUNT DAW AND MAVIS.]

CLER: He has it in the haft of a knife, I believe.

LA-F: No, he has his box of instruments.

CLER: Like a surgeon!

LA-F: For the mathematics: his square, his compasses, his brass

97

pens, and black-lead, to draw maps of every place and person where he comes.

CLER: How, maps of persons!

LA-F: Yes, sir, of Nomentack when he was here, and of the Prince of Moldavia, and of his mistress, mistress Epicoene.

[RE-ENTER DAW.]

CLER: Away! he hath not found out her latitude, I hope.

LA-F: You are a pleasant gentleman, sir.

CLER: Faith, now we are in private, let's wanton it a little, and talk waggishly.—Sir John, I am telling sir Amorous here, that you two govern the ladies wherever you come; you carry the feminine gender afore you.

DAW: They shall rather carry us afore them, if they will, sir.

CLER: Nay, I believe that they do, withal—but that you are the prime men in their affections, and direct all their actions—

DAW: Not I: sir Amorous is.

LA-F: I protest, sir John is.

DAW: As I hope to rise in the state, sir Amorous, you have the person.

LA-F: Sir John, you have the person, and the discourse too.

DAW: Not I, sir. I have no discourse—and then you have activity beside.

LA-F: I protest, sir John, you come as high from Tripoly as I do, every whit: and lift as many join'd stools, and leap over them, if you would use it.

CLER: Well, agree on't together knights; for between you, you divide the kingdom or commonwealth of ladies' affections: I see it, and can perceive a little how they observe you, and fear you,

98

indeed. You could tell strange stories, my masters, if you would, I know.

DAW: Faith, we have seen somewhat, sir.

LA-F: That we have—velvet petticoats, and wrought smocks, or so.

DAW: Ay, and—

CLER: Nay, out with it, sir John: do not envy your friend the pleasure of hearing, when you have had the delight of tasting.

DAW: Why—a—do you speak, sir Amorous.

LA-F: No, do you, sir John Daw.

DAW: I'faith, you shall.

LA-F: I'faith, you shall.

DAW: Why, we have been—

LA-F: In the great bed at Ware together in our time. On, sir John.

DAW: Nay, do you, sir Amorous.

CLER: And these ladies with you, knights?

LA-F: No, excuse us, sir.

DAW: We must not wound reputation.

LA-F: No matter—they were these, or others. Our bath cost us fifteen pound when we came home.

CLER: Do you hear, sir John? You shall tell me but one thing truly, as you love me.

DAW: If I can, I will, sir.

CLER: You lay in the same house with the bride, here?

DAW: Yes, and conversed with her hourly, sir.

CLER: And what humour is she of? Is she coming, and open, free?

DAW: O, exceeding open, sir. I was her servant, and sir Amorous was to be.

CLER: Come, you have both had favours from her: I know, and have heard so much.

DAW: O no, sir.

LA-F: You shall excuse us, sir: we must not wound reputation.

CLER: Tut, she is married now, and you cannot hurt her with any report; and therefore speak plainly: how many times, i'faith? which of you led first? ha!

LA-F: Sir John had her maidenhead, indeed.

DAW: O, it pleases him to say so, sir, but sir Amorous knows what is what, as well.

CLER: Dost thou i'faith, Amorous?

LA-F: In a manner, sir.

CLER: Why, I commend you lads. Little knows don Bridegroom of this. Nor shall he, for me.

DAW: Hang him, mad ox!

CLER: Speak softly: here comes his nephew, with the lady Haughty. He'll get the ladies from you, sirs, if you look not to him in time.

LA-F: Why, if he do, we'll fetch them home again, I warrant you.

[EXIT WITH DAW. CLER. WALKS ASIDE.]

[ENTER DAUPHINE AND HAUGHTY.]

HAU: I assure you, sir Dauphine, it is the price and estimation of your virtue only, that hath embark'd me to this adventure; and I could not but make out to tell you so; nor can I repent me of the act, since it is always an argument of some virtue in our selves, that we love and affect it so in others.

DAUP: Your ladyship sets too high a price on my weakness.

HAU: Sir, I can distinguish gems from pebbles—

DAUP [ASIDE.]: Are you so skilful in stones?

HAU: And howsover I may suffer in such a judgment as yours, by admitting equality of rank or society with Centaure or Mavis—

DAUP: You do not, madam; I perceive they are your mere foils.

HAU: Then, are you a friend to truth, sir; it makes me love you the more. It is not the outward, but the inward man that I affect. They are not apprehensive of an eminent perfection, but love flat, and dully.

CEN [within.]: Where are you, my lady Haughty?

HAU: I come presently, Centaure.—My chamber, sir, my page shall shew you; and Trusty, my woman, shall be ever awake for you: you need not fear to communicate any thing with her, for she is a Fidelia. I pray you wear this jewel for my sake, sir Dauphine.—
[ENTER CENTAURE.]
Where is Mavis, Centaure?

CEN: Within, madam, a writing. I'll follow you presently:
[EXIT HAU.]
I'll but speak a word with sir Dauphine.

DAUP: With me, madam?

CEN: Good sir Dauphine, do not trust Haughty, nor make any credit to her, whatever you do besides. Sir Dauphine, I give you this caution, she is a perfect courtier, and loves nobody but for her uses: and for her uses she loves all. Besides, her physicians give her out to be none o' the clearest, whether she pay them or no, heaven knows: and she's above fifty too, and pargets! See her in a forenoon. Here comes Mavis, a worse face then she! you would not like this, by candle-light.
[RE-ENTER MAVIS.]

If you'll come to my chamber one o' these mornings early, or late in an evening, I will tell you more. Where's Haughty, Mavis?

MAV: Within, Centaure.

CEN: What have you, there?

MAV: An Italian riddle for sir Dauphine,—you shall not see it i'faith, Centaure.—
[EXIT CEN.]
Good sir Dauphine, solve it for me. I'll call for it anon.

[EXIT.]

CLER [COMING FORWARD.]: How now, Dauphine! how dost thou quit thyself of these females?

DAUP: 'Slight, they haunt me like fairies, and give me jewels here; I cannot be rid of them.

CLER: O, you must not tell though.

DAUP: Mass, I forgot that: I was never so assaulted. One loves for virtue, and bribes me with this;
[SHEWS THE JEWEL.]
—another loves me with caution, and so would possess me; a third brings me a riddle here: and all are jealous: and rail each at other.

CLER: A riddle! pray let me see it.
[READS.]
Sir Dauphine, I chose this way of intimation for privacy. The ladies here, I know, have both hope and purpose to make a collegiate and servant of you. If I might be so honoured, as to appear at any end of so noble a work, I would enter into a fame of taking physic to-morrow, and continue it four or five days, or longer, for your visitation. Mavis.
By my faith, a subtle one! Call you this a riddle? what's their plain dealing, trow?

DAUP: We lack Truewit to tell us that.

CLER: We lack him for somewhat else too: his knights reformadoes are wound up as high and insolent as ever they were.

102

DAUP: You jest.

CLER: No drunkards, either with wine or vanity, ever confess'd
such stories of themselves. I would not give a fly's leg, in
balance against all the womens' reputations here, if they could
be but thought to speak truth: and for the bride, they have made
their affidavit against her directly—

DAUP: What, that they have lain with her?

CLER: Yes; and tell times and circumstances, with the cause why,
and the place where. I had almost brought them to affirm that
they had done it to-day.

DAUP: Not both of them?

CLER: Yes, faith: with a sooth or two more I had effected it.
They would have set it down under their hands.

DAUP: Why, they will be our sport, I see, still, whether we will
or no.

[ENTER TRUEWIT.]

TRUE: O, are you here? Come, Dauphine; go call your uncle
presently: I have fitted my divine, and my canonist, dyed
their beards and all. The knaves do not know themselves, they
are so exalted and altered. Preferment changes any man. Thou
shalt keep one door and I another, and then Clerimont in the
midst, that he may have no means of escape from their cavilling,
when they grow hot once again. And then the women, as I have
given the bride her instructions, to break in upon him in the
l'enuoy. O, 'twill be full and twanging! Away! fetch him.
[EXIT DAUPHINE.]
[ENTER OTTER DISGUISED AS A DIVINE, AND CUTBEARD AS
A CANON LAWYER.]
Come, master doctor, and master parson, look to your parts now,
and discharge them bravely: you are well set forth, perform it
as well. If you chance to be out, do not confess it with standing
still, or humming, or gaping one at another: but go on, and talk
aloud and eagerly; use vehement action, and only remember your
terms, and you are safe. Let the matter go where it will: you
have many will do so. But at first be very solemn, and grave like
your garments, though you loose your selves after, and skip out

103

like a brace of jugglers on a table. Here he comes: set your faces, and look superciliously, while I present you.

[RE-ENTER DAUPHINE WITH MOROSE.]

MOR: Are these the two learned men?

TRUE: Yes, sir; please you salute them.

MOR: Salute them! I had rather do any thing, than wear out time so unfruitfully, sir. I wonder how these common forms, as God save you, and You are welcome, are come to be a habit in our lives: or, I am glad to see you! when I cannot see what the profit can be of these words, so long as it is no whit better with him whose affairs are sad and grievous, that he hears this salutation.

TRUE: 'Tis true, sir; we'll go to the matter then.—Gentlemen, master doctor, and master parson, I have acquainted you sufficiently with the business for which you are come hither; and you are not now to inform yourselves in the state of the question, I know. This is the gentleman who expects your resolution, and therefore, when you please, begin.

OTT: Please you, master doctor.

CUT: Please you, good master parson.

OTT: I would hear the canon-law speak first.

CUT: It must give place to positive divinity, sir.

MOR: Nay, good gentlemen, do not throw me into circumstances. Let your comforts arrive quickly at me, those that are. Be swift in affording me my peace, if so I shall hope any. I love not your disputations, or your court-tumults. And that it be not strange to you, I will tell you: My father, in my education, was wont to advise me, that I should always collect and contain my mind, not suffering it to flow loosely; that I should look to what things were necessary to the carriage of my life, and what not; embracing the one and eschewing the other: in short, that I should endear myself to rest, and avoid turmoil: which now is grown to be another nature to me. So that I come not to your public pleadings, or your places of noise; not that I neglect those things that make for the dignity of the commonwealth: but for the mere avoiding of clamours and impertinencies of orators, that know not how to be silent. And for the cause of noise, am I now a suitor to you. You do not know in what a misery I have been exercised this day, what a torrent of evil! my very house turns round with the tumult! I dwell in a windmill: The perpetual motion is here, and not at Eltham.

TRUE: Well, good master doctor, will you break the ice? master parson will wade after.

CUT: Sir, though unworthy, and the weaker, I will presume.

OTT: 'Tis no presumption, domine doctor.

MOR: Yet again!

CUT: Your question is, For how many causes a man may have divortium legitimum, a lawful divorce? First, you must understand the nature of the word, divorce, a divertendo—

MOR: No excursions upon words, good doctor, to the question briefly.

CUT: I answer then, the canon-law affords divorce but in a few cases; and the principal is in the common case, the adulterous case: But there are duodecim impedimenta, twelve impediments, as we call them, all which do not dirimere contractum, but irritum reddere matrimonium, as we say in the canon-law, not take away the bond, but cause a nullity therein.

MOR: I understood you before: good sir, avoid your impertinency of translation.

OTT: He cannot open this too much, sir, by your favour.

MOR: Yet more!

TRUE: O, you must give the learned men leave, sir.—To your impediments, master Doctor.

CUT: The first is impedimentum erroris.

OTT: Of which there are several species.

105

CUT: Ay, as error personae.

OTT: If you contract yourself to one person, thinking her another.

CUT: Then, error fortunae.

OTT: If she be a begger, and you thought her rich.

CUT: Then, error qualitatis.

OTT: If she prove stubborn or head-strong, that you thought obedient.

MOR: How! is that, sir, a lawful impediment? One at once, I pray you gentlemen.

OTT: Ay, ante copulam, but not post copulam, sir.

CUT: Master Parson says right. Nec post nuptiarum benedictionem. It doth indeed but irrita reddere sponsalia, annul the contract: after marriage it is of no obstancy.

TRUE: Alas, sir, what a hope are we fallen from by this time!

CUT: The next is conditio: if you thought her free born, and she prove a bond-woman, there is impediment of estate and condition.

OTT: Ay, but, master doctor, those servitudes are sublatae now, among us Christians.

CUT: By your favour, master parson—

OTT: You shall give me leave, master doctor.

MOR: Nay, gentlemen, quarrel not in that question; it concerns not my case: pass to the third.

CUT: Well then, the third is votum: if either party have made a vow of chastity. But that practice, as master parson said of the other, is taken away among us, thanks be to discipline. The fourth is cognatio: if the persons be of kin within the degrees.

OTT: Ay: do you know what the degrees are, sir?

106

MOR: No, nor I care not, sir: they offer me no comfort in the question, I am sure.

CUT: But there is a branch of this impediment may, which is cognatio spiritualis: if you were her godfather, sir, then the marriage is incestuous.

OTT: That comment is absurd and superstitious, master doctor: I cannot endure it. Are we not all brothers and sisters, and as much akin in that, as godfathers and god-daughters?

MOR: O me! to end the controversy, I never was a godfather, I never was a godfather in my life, sir. Pass to the next.

CUT: The fifth is crimen adulterii; the known case. The sixth, cultus disparitas, difference of religion: have you ever examined her, what religion she is of?

MOR: No, I would rather she were of none, than be put to the trouble of it!

OTT: You may have it done for you, sir.

MOR: By no means, good sir; on to the rest: shall you ever come to an end, think you?

TRUE: Yes, he has done half, sir. On, to the rest.—Be patient, and expect, sir.

CUT: The seventh is, vis: if it were upon compulsion or force.

MOR: O no, it was too voluntary, mine; too voluntary.

CUT: The eight is, ordo; if ever she have taken holy orders.

OTT: That's supersitious too.

MOR: No matter, master parson: Would she would go into a nunnery yet.

CUT: The ninth is, ligamen; if you were bound, sir, to any other before.

MOR: I thrust myself too soon into these fetters.

CUT: The tenth is, publica honestas: which is inchoata quaedam affinitas.

OTT: Ay, or affinitas orta ex sponsalibus; and is but leve impedimentum.

MOR: I feel no air of comfort blowing to me, in all this.

CUT: The eleventh is, affinitas ex fornicatione.

OTT: Which is no less vera affinitas, than the other, master doctor.

CUT: True, quae oritur ex legitimo matrimonio.

OTT: You say right, venerable doctor: and, nascitur ex eo, quod per conjugium duae personae efficiuntur una caro—

MOR: Hey-day, now they begin!

CUT: I conceive you, master parson: ita per fornicationem aeque est verus pater, qui sic generat—

OTT: Et vere filius qui sic generatur—

MOR: What's all this to me?

CLER: Now it grows warm.

CUT: The twelfth, and last is, si forte coire nequibis.

OTT: Ay, that is impedimentum gravissimum: it doth utterly annul, and annihilate, that. If you have manifestam frigiditatem, you are well, sir.

TRUE: Why, there is comfort come at length, sir. Confess yourself but a man unable, and she will sue to be divorced first.

OTT: Ay, or if there be morbus perpetuus, et insanabilis; as paralysis, elephantiasis, or so—

DAUP: O, but frigiditas is the fairer way, gentlemen.

OTT: You say troth, sir, and as it is in the canon, master doctor—

CUT: I conceive you, sir.

CLER: Before he speaks!

OTT: That a boy, or child, under years, is not fit for marriage, because he cannot reddere debitum. So your omnipotentes—

TRUE [ASIDE TO OTT.]: Your impotentes, you whoreson lobster!

OTT: Your impotentes, I should say, are minime apti ad contrahenda matrimonium.

TRUE: Matrimonium! we shall have most unmatrimonial Latin with you: matrimonia, and be hang'd.

DAUP: You put them out, man.

CUT: But then there will arise a doubt, master parson, in our case, post matrimonium: that frigiditate praeditus—do you conceive me, sir?

OTT: Very well, sir.

CUT: Who cannot uti uxore pro uxore, may habere eam pro sorore.

OTT: Absurd, absurd, absurd, and merely apostatical!

CUT: You shall pardon me, master parson, I can prove it.

OTT: You can prove a will, master doctor, you can prove nothing else. Does not the verse of your own canon say, Haec socianda vetant connubia, facta retractant?

CUT: I grant you; but how do they retractare, master parson?

MOR: O, this was it I feared.

OTT: In aeternum, sir.

CUT: That's false in divinity, by your favour.

OTT: 'Tis false in humanity to say so. Is he not prorsus inutilis ad thorum? Can he praestare fidem datam? I would fain know.

109

CUT: Yes; how if he do convalere?

OTT: He cannot convalere, it is impossible.

TRUE: Nay, good sir, attend the learned men, they will think you neglect them else.

CUT: Or, if he do simulare himself frigidum, odio uxoris, or so?

OTT: I say, he is adulter manifestus then.

DAUP: They dispute it very learnedly, i'faith.

OTT: And prostitutor uxoris; and this is positive.

MOR: Good sir, let me escape.

TRUE: You will not do me that wrong, sir?

OTT: And, therefore, if he be manifeste frigidus, sir—

CUT: Ay, if he be manifeste frigidus, I grant you—

OTT: Why, that was my conclusion.

CUT: And mine too.

TRUE: Nay, hear the conclusion, sir.

OTT: Then, frigiditatis causa—

CUT: Yes, causa frigiditatis—

MOR: O, mine ears!

OTT: She may have libellum divortii against you.

CUT: Ay, divortii libellum she will sure have.

MOR: Good echoes, forbear.

OTT: If you confess it.

CUT: Which I would do, sir—

110

MOR: I will do any thing.

OTT: And clear myself in foro conscientiae—

CUT: Because you want indeed—

MOR: Yet more?

OTT: Exercendi potestate.

[EPICOENE RUSHES IN, FOLLOWED BY HAUGHTY, CENTAURE, MAVIS, MISTRESS OTTER, DAW, AND LA-FOOLE.]

EPI: I will not endure it any longer. Ladies, I beseech you, help me. This is such a wrong as never was offered to poor bride before: upon her marriage day, to have her husband conspire against her, and a couple of mercenary companions to be brought in for form's sake, to persuade a separation! If you had blood or virtue in you, gentlemen, you would not suffer such ear-wigs about a husband, or scorpions to creep between man and wife.

MOR: O the variety and changes of my torment!

HAU: Let them be cudgell'd out of doors, by our grooms.

CEN: I'll lend you my foot-man.

MAV: We'll have our men blanket them in the hall.

MRS. OTT: As there was one at our house, madam, for peeping in at the door.

DAW: Content, i'faith.

TRUE: Stay, ladies and gentlemen; you'll hear, before you proceed?

MAV: I'd have the bridegroom blanketted too.

CEN: Begin with him first.

HAU: Yes, by my troth.

111

MOR: O mankind generation!

DAUP: Ladies, for my sake forbear.

HAU: Yes, for sir Dauphine's sake.

CEN: He shall command us.

LA-F: He is as fine a gentleman of his inches, madam, as any is about the town, and wears as good colours when he lists.

TRUE: Be brief, sir, and confess your infirmity, she'll be a-fire to be quit of you, if she but hear that named once, you shall not entreat her to stay: she'll fly you like one that had the marks upon him.

MOR: Ladies, I must crave all your pardons—

TRUE: Silence, ladies.

MOR: For a wrong I have done to your whole sex, in marrying this fair, and virtuous gentlewoman—

CLER: Hear him, good ladies.

MOR: Being guilty of an infirmity, which, before I conferred with these learned men, I thought I might have concealed—

TRUE: But now being better informed in his conscience by them, he is to declare it, and give satisfaction, by asking your public forgiveness.

MOR: I am no man, ladies.

ALL: How!

MOR: Utterly unabled in nature, by reason of frigidity, to perform the duties, or any the least office of a husband.

MAV: Now out upon him, prodigious creature!

CEN: Bridegroom uncarnate!

HAU: And would you offer it to a young gentlewoman?

112

MRS. OTT: A lady of her longings?

EPI: Tut, a device, a device, this, it smells rankly, ladies. A mere comment of his own.

TRUE: Why, if you suspect that, ladies, you may have him search'd—

DAW: As the custom is, by a jury of physicians.

LA-F: Yes faith, 'twill be brave.

MOR: O me, must I undergo that?

MRS. OTT: No, let women search him, madam: we can do it ourselves.

MOR: Out on me! worse.

EPI: No, ladies, you shall not need, I will take him with all his faults.

MOR: Worst of all!

CLER: Why then, 'tis no divorce, doctor, if she consent not?

CUT: No, if the man be frigidus, it is de parte uxoris, that we grant libellum divortii, in the law.

OTT: Ay, it is the same in theology.

MOR: Worse, worse than worst!

TRUE: Nay, sir, be not utterly disheartened; we have yet a small relic of hope left, as near as our comfort is blown out. Clerimont, produce your brace of knights. What was that, master parson, you told me in errore qualitatis, e'en now?—
[ASIDE.]
Dauphine, whisper the bride, that she carry it as if she were guilty, and ashamed.

OTT: Marry, sir, in errore qualitatis (which master doctor did forbear to urge,) if she be found corrupta, that is, vitiated or broken up, that was pro virgine desponsa, espoused for a maid—

MOR: What then, sir?

OTT: It doth dirimere contractum, and irritum reddere too.

TRUE: If this be true, we are happy again, sir, once more. Here are an honourable brace of knights, that shall affirm so much.

DAW: Pardon us, good master Clerimont.

LA-F: You shall excuse us, master Clerimont.

CLER: Nay, you must make it good now, knights, there is no remedy; I'll eat no words for you, nor no men: you know you spoke it to me.

DAW: Is this gentleman-like, sir?

TRUE [ASIDE TO DAW.]: Jack Daw, he's worse then sir Amorous; fiercer a great deal.
[ASIDE TO LA-FOOLE.]—Sir Amorous, beware, there be ten Daws in this Clerimont.

LA-F: I'll confess it, sir.

DAW: Will you, sir Amorous, will you wound reputation?

LA-F: I am resolved.

TRUE: So should you be too, Jack Daw: what should keep you off? she's but a woman, and in disgrace: he'll be glad on't.

DAW: Will he? I thought he would have been angry.

CLER: You will dispatch, knights, it must be done, i'faith.

TRUE: Why, an it must, it shall, sir, they say: they'll ne'er go back.
[ASIDE TO THEM.]
—Do not tempt his patience.

DAW: It is true indeed, sir?

LA-F: Yes, I assure you, sir.

114

MOR: What is true gentlemen? what do you assure me?

DAW: That we have known your bride, sir—

LA-F: In good fashion. She was our mistress, or so—

CLER: Nay, you must be plain, knights, as you were to me.

OTT: Ay, the question is, if you have carnaliter, or no?

LA-F: Carnaliter! what else, sir?

OTT: It is enough: a plain nullity.

EPI: I am undone, I am undone!

MOR: O, let me worship and adore you, gentlemen!

EPI [WEEPS.]: I am undone!

MOR: Yes, to my hand, I thank these knights.
Master parson, let me thank you otherwise. [GIVES HIM
MONEY.]

HAU: And have they confess'd?

MAV: Now out upon them, informers!

TRUE: You see what creatures you may bestow your favours
on, madams.

HAU: I would except against them as beaten knights, wench,
and not good witnesses in law.

MRS. OTT: Poor gentlewoman, how she takes it!

HAU: Be comforted, Morose, I love you the better for't.

CEN: so do I, I protest.

CUT: But, gentlemen, you have not known her since
matrimonium?

DAW: Not to-day, master doctor.

LA-F: No, sir, not to-day.

CUT: Why, then I say, for any act before, the matrimonium is good and perfect: unless the worshipful bridegroom did precisely, before witness, demand, if she were virgo ante nuptias.

EPI: No, that he did not, I assure you, master doctor.

CUT: If he cannot prove that, it is ratum conjugium, notwithstanding the premises. And they do no way impedire. And this is my sentence, this I pronounce.

OTT: I am of master doctor's resolution too, sir: if you made not that demand, ante nuptias.

MOR: O my heart! wilt thou break? wilt thou break? this is worst of all worst worsts that hell could have devised! Marry a whore, and so much noise!

DAUP: Come, I see now plain confederacy in this doctor and this parson, to abuse a gentleman. You study his affliction. I pray be gone companions.—And, gentlemen, I begin to suspect you for having parts with them.—Sir, will it please you hear me?

MOR: O do not talk to me, take not from me the pleasure of dying in silence, nephew.

DAUP: Sir, I must speak to you. I have been long your poor despised kinsman, and many a hard thought has strengthened you against me: but now it shall appear if either I love you or your peace, and prefer them to all the world beside. I will not be long or grievous to you, sir. If I free you of this unhappy match absolutely, and instantly, after all this trouble, and almost in your despair, now—

MOR: It cannot be.

DAUP: Sir, that you be never troubled with a murmur of it more, what shall I hope for, or deserve of you?

MOR: O, what thou wilt, nephew! thou shalt deserve me, and have me.

DAUP: Shall I have your favour perfect to me, and love hereafter?

116

MOR: That, and any thing beside. Make thine own conditions. My whole estate is thine; manage it, I will become thy ward.

DAUP: Nay, sir, I will not be so unreasonable.

EPI: Will sir Dauphine be mine enemy too?

DAUP: You know I have been long a suitor to you, uncle, that out of your estate, which is fifteen hundred a-year, you would allow me but five hundred during life, and assure the rest upon me after: to which I have often, by myself and friends tendered you a writing to sign, which you would never consent or incline to. If you please but to effect it now—

MOR: Thou shalt have it, nephew: I will do it, and more.

DAUP: If I quit you not presently, and for ever of this cumber, you shall have power instantly, afore all these, to revoke your act, and I will become whose slave you will give me to, for ever.

MOR: Where is the writing? I will seal to it, that, or to a blank, and write thine own conditions.

EPI: O me, most unfortunate, wretched gentlewoman!

HAU: Will sir Dauphine do this?

EPI: Good sir, have some compassion on me.

MOR: O, my nephew knows you, belike; away, crocodile!

HAU: He does it not sure without good ground.

DAUP: Here, sir. [GIVES HIM THE PARCHMENTS.]

MOR: Come, nephew, give me the pen. I will subscribe to any thing, and seal to what thou wilt, for my deliverance. Thou art my restorer. Here, I deliver it thee as my deed. If there be a word in it lacking, or writ with false orthography, I protest before [heaven] I will not take the advantage.
[RETURNS THE WRITINGS.]

DAUP: Then here is your release, sir.

117

[TAKES OFF EPICOENE'S PERUKE AND OTHER DISGUISES.]
You have married a boy, a gentleman's son, that I have
brought up this half year at my great charges, and for this
composition, which I have now made with you.—What say you,
master doctor? This is justum impedimentum, I hope, error
personae?

OTT: Yes sir, in primo gradu.

CUT: In primo gradu.

DAUP: I thank you, good doctor Cutbeard, and parson Otter.
[PULLS THEIR FALSE BEARDS AND GOWNS OFF.]
You are beholden to them, sir, that have taken this pains for
you; and my friend, master Truewit, who enabled them for the
business. Now you may go in and rest; be as private as you
will, sir.
[EXIT MOROSE.]
I'll not trouble you, till you trouble me with your funeral,
which I care not how soon it come.
—Cutbeard, I'll make your lease good. "Thank me not, but with
your leg, Cutbeard." And Tom Otter, your princess shall be
reconciled to you.—How now, gentlemen, do you look at me?

CLER: A boy!

DAUP: Yes, mistress Epicoene.

TRUE: Well, Dauphine, you have lurch'd your friends of the
better half of the garland, by concealing this part of the
plot: but much good do it thee, thou deserv'st it, lad. And,
Clerimont, for thy unexpected bringing these two to
confession, wear my part of it freely. Nay, sir Daw, and sir
La-Foole, you see the gentlewoman that has done you the
favours! we are all thankful to you, and so should the
woman-kind here, specially for lying on her, though not
with her! you meant so, I am sure? But that we have stuck it
upon you to-day, in your own imagined persons, and so lately,
this Amazon, the champion of the sex, should beat you now
thriftily, for the common slanders which ladies receive from
such cuckoos as you are. You are they that, when no merit or
fortune can make you hope to enjoy their bodies, will yet
lie with their reputations, and make their fame suffer. Away,
you common moths of these, and all ladies' honours. Go,

118

travel to make legs and faces, and come home with some new
matter to be laugh'd at: you deserve to live in an air as
corrupted as that wherewith you feed rumour.
[EXEUNT DAW AND LA-FOOLE.]
Madams, you are mute, upon this new metamorphosis! But here
stands she that has vindicated your fames. Take heed of such
insectae hereafter. And let it not trouble you, that you
have discovered any mysteries to this young gentleman: he is
almost of years, and will make a good visitant within this
twelvemonth. In the mean time, we'll all undertake for his
secrecy, that can speak so well of his silence.
[COMING FORWARD.]
—Spectators, if you like this comedy, rise cheerfully, and
now Morose is gone in, clap your hands. It may be, that noise
will cure him, at least please him.
[EXEUNT.]

119

GLOSSARY

ABATE, cast down, subdue.

ABHORRING, repugnant (to), at variance.

ABJECT, base, degraded thing, outcast.

ABRASE, smooth, blank.

ABSOLUTE(LY), faultless(ly).

ABSTRACTED, abstract, abstruse.

ABUSE, deceive, insult, dishonour, make ill use of.

ACATER, caterer.

ACATES, cates.

ACCEPTIVE, willing, ready to accept, receive.

ACCOMMODATE, fit, befitting. (The word was a fashionable one and used on all occasions. See "Henry IV.," pt. 2, iii. 4).

ACCOST, draw near, approach.

ACKNOWN, confessedly acquainted with.

ACME, full maturity.

ADALANTADO, lord deputy or governor of a Spanish province.

ADJECTION, addition.

ADMIRATION, astonishment.

ADMIRE, wonder, wonder at.

ADROP, philosopher's stone, or substance from which obtained.

ADSCRIVE, subscribe.

ADULTERATE, spurious, counterfeit.

ADVANCE, lift.

ADVERTISE, inform, give intelligence.

ADVERTISED, "be —," be it known to you.

ADVERTISEMENT, intelligence.

ADVISE, consider, bethink oneself, deliberate.

ADVISED, informed, aware; "are you —?" have you found that out?

AFFECT, love, like; aim at; move.

AFFECTED, disposed; beloved.

AFFECTIONATE, obstinate; prejudiced.

AFFECTS, affections.

AFFRONT, "give the —," face.

AFFY, have confidence in; betroth.

AFTER, after the manner of.

AGAIN, AGAINST, in anticipation of.

AGGRAVATE, increase, magnify, enlarge upon.

AGNOMINATION. See Paranomasie.

AIERY, nest, brood.

AIM, guess.

ALL HID, children's cry at hide-and-seek.

ALL-TO, completely, entirely ("all-to-be-laden").

ALLOWANCE, approbation, recognition.

121

ALMA-CANTARAS (astronomy), parallels of altitude.

ALMAIN, name of a dance.

ALMUTEN, planet of chief influence in the horoscope.

ALONE, unequalled, without peer.

ALUDELS, subliming pots.

AMAZED, confused, perplexed.

AMBER, AMBRE, ambergris.

AMBREE, MARY, a woman noted for her valour at the siege of Ghent, 1458.

AMES-ACE, lowest throw at dice.

AMPHIBOLIES, ambiguities.

AMUSED, bewildered, amazed.

AN, if.

ANATOMY, skeleton, or dissected body.

ANDIRONS, fire-dogs.

ANGEL, gold coin worth 10 shillings, stamped with the figure of the archangel Michael.

ANNESH CLEARE, spring known as Agnes le Clare.

ANSWER, return hit in fencing.

ANTIC, ANTIQUE, clown, buffoon.

ANTIC, like a buffoon.

ANTIPERISTASIS, an opposition which enhances the quality it opposes.

APOZEM, decoction.

APPERIL, peril.

APPLE-JOHN, APPLE-SQUIRE, pimp, pander.

APPLY, attach.

APPREHEND, take into custody.

APPREHENSIVE, quick of perception; able to perceive and appreciate.

APPROVE, prove, confirm.

APT, suit, adapt; train, prepare; dispose, incline.

APT(LY), suitable(y), opportune(ly).

APTITUDE, suitableness.

ARBOR, "make the —," cut up the game (Gifford).

ARCHES, Court of Arches.

ARCHIE, Archibald Armstrong, jester to James I. and Charles I.

ARGAILE, argol, crust or sediment in wine casks.

ARGENT-VIVE, quicksilver.

ARGUMENT, plot of a drama; theme, subject; matter in question; token, proof.

ARRIDE, please.

ARSEDINE, mixture of copper and zinc, used as an imitation of gold-leaf.

ARTHUR, PRINCE, reference to an archery show by a society who assumed arms, etc., of Arthur's knights.

ARTICLE, item.

ARTIFICIALLY, artfully.

ASCENSION, evaporation, distillation.

ASPIRE, try to reach, obtain, long for.

ASSALTO (Italian), assault.

ASSAY, draw a knife along the belly of the deer, a ceremony of the hunting-field.

ASSOIL, solve.

ASSURE, secure possession or reversion of.

ATHANOR, a digesting furnace, calculated to keep up a constant heat.

ATONE, reconcile.

ATTACH, attack, seize.

AUDACIOUS, having spirit and confidence.

AUTHENTIC(AL), of authority, authorised, trustworthy, genuine.

AVISEMENT, reflection, consideration.

AVOID, begone! get rid of.

AWAY WITH, endure.

AZOCH, Mercurius Philosophorum.

BABION, baboon.

BABY, doll.

BACK-SIDE, back premises.

BAFFLE, treat with contempt.

BAGATINE, Italian coin, worth about the third of a farthing.

BAIARD, horse of magic powers known to old romance.

BALDRICK, belt worn across the breast to support bugle, etc.

BALE (of dice), pair.

BALK, overlook, pass by, avoid.

BALLACE, ballast.

BALLOO, game at ball.

BALNEUM (BAIN MARIE), a vessel for holding hot water in which other vessels are stood for heating.

BANBURY, "brother of —," Puritan.

BANDOG, dog tied or chained up.

BANE, woe, ruin.

BANQUET, a light repast; dessert.

BARB, to clip gold.

BARBEL, fresh-water fish.

BARE, meer; bareheaded; it was "a particular mark of state and grandeur for the coachman to be uncovered" (Gifford).

BARLEY-BREAK, game somewhat similar to base.

BASE, game of prisoner's base.

BASES, richly embroidered skirt reaching to the knees, or lower.

BASILISK, fabulous reptile, believed to slay with its eye.

BASKET, used for the broken provision collected for prisoners.

BASON, basons, etc., were beaten by the attendant mob when bad characters were "carted."

BATE, be reduced; abate, reduce.

BATOON, baton, stick.

BATTEN, feed, grow fat.

BAWSON, badger.

BEADSMAN, prayer-man, one engaged to pray for another.

BEAGLE, small hound; fig. spy.

BEAR IN HAND, keep in suspense, deceive with false hopes.

BEARWARD, bear leader.

BEDPHERE. See Phere.

BEDSTAFF, (?) wooden pin in the side of the bedstead for supporting the bedclothes (Johnson); one of the sticks or "laths"; a stick used in making a bed.

BEETLE, heavy mallet.

BEG, "I'd — him," the custody of minors and idiots was begged for; likewise property fallen forfeit to the Crown ("your house had been begged").

BELL-MAN, night watchman.

BENJAMIN, an aromatic gum.

BERLINA, pillory.

BESCUMBER, defile.

BESLAVE, beslabber.

BESOGNO, beggar.

BESPAWLE, bespatter.

BETHLEHEM GABOR, Transylvanian hero, proclaimed King of Hungary.

BEVER, drinking.

126

BEVIS, SIR, knight of romance whose horse was equally celebrated.

BEWRAY, reveal, make known.

BEZANT, heraldic term: small gold circle.

BEZOAR'S STONE, a remedy known by this name was a supposed antidote to poison.

BID-STAND, highwayman.

BIGGIN, cap, similar to that worn by the Beguines; nightcap.

BILIVE (belive), with haste.

BILK, nothing, empty talk.

BILL, kind of pike.

BILLET, wood cut for fuel, stick.

BIRDING, thieving.

BLACK SANCTUS, burlesque hymn, any unholy riot.

BLANK, originally a small French coin.

BLANK, white.

BLANKET, toss in a blanket.

BLAZE, outburst of violence.

BLAZE, (her.) blazon; publish abroad.

BLAZON, armorial bearings; fig. all that pertains to good birth and breeding.

BLIN, "withouten —," without ceasing.

BLOW, puff up.

BLUE, colour of servants' livery, hence "— order," "— waiters."

BLUSHET, blushing one.

BOB, jest, taunt.

BOB, beat, thump.

BODGE, measure.

BODKIN, dagger, or other short, pointed weapon; long pin with which the women fastened up their hair.

BOLT, roll (of material).

BOLT, dislodge, rout out; sift (boulting-tub).

BOLT'S-HEAD, long, straight-necked vessel for distillation.

BOMBARD SLOPS, padded, puffed-out breeches.

BONA ROBA, "good, wholesome, plum-cheeked wench" (Johnson) — not always used in compliment.

BONNY-CLABBER, sour butter-milk.

BOOKHOLDER, prompter.

BOOT, "to —," into the bargain; "no —," of no avail.

BORACHIO, bottle made of skin.

BORDELLO, brothel.

BORNE IT, conducted, carried it through.

BOTTLE (of hay), bundle, truss.

BOTTOM, skein or ball of thread; vessel.

BOURD, jest.

BOVOLI, snails or cockles dressed in the Italian manner (Gifford).

BOW-POT, flower vase or pot.

BOYS, "terrible —," "angry —," roystering young bucks.
(See Nares).

BRABBLES (BRABBLESH), brawls.

BRACH, bitch.

BRADAMANTE, a heroine in "Orlando Furioso."

BRADLEY, ARTHUR OF, a lively character commemorated in
ballads.

BRAKE, frame for confining a horse's feet while being shod, or
strong curb or bridle; trap.

BRANCHED, with "detached sleeve ornaments, projecting
from the shoulders of the gown" (Gifford).

BRANDISH, flourish of weapon.

BRASH, brace.

BRAVE, bravado, braggart speech.

BRAVE (adv.), gaily, finely (apparelled).

BRAVERIES, gallants.

BRAVERY, extravagant gaiety of apparel.

BRAVO, bravado, swaggerer.

BRAZEN-HEAD, speaking head made by Roger Bacon.

BREATHE, pause for relaxation; exercise.

BREATH UPON, speak dispraisingly of.

BREND, burn.

BRIDE-ALE, wedding feast.

BRIEF, abstract; (mus.) breve.

129

BRISK, smartly dressed.

BRIZE, breese, gadfly.

BROAD-SEAL, state seal.

BROCK, badger (term of contempt).

BROKE, transact business as a broker.

BROOK, endure, put up with.

BROUGHTON, HUGH, an English divine and Hebrew scholar.

BRUIT, rumour.

BUCK, wash.

BUCKLE, bend.

BUFF, leather made of buffalo skin, used for military and serjeants' coats, etc.

BUFO, black tincture.

BUGLE, long-shaped bead.

BULLED, (?) bolled, swelled.

BULLIONS, trunk hose.

BULLY, term of familiar endearment.

BUNGY, Friar Bungay, who had a familiar in the shape of a dog.

BURDEN, refrain, chorus.

BURGONET, closely-fitting helmet with visor.

BURGULLION, braggadocio.

BURN, mark wooden measures ("—ing of cans").

BURROUGH, pledge, security.

BUSKIN, half-boot, foot gear reaching high up the leg.

BUTT-SHAFT, barbless arrow for shooting at butts.

BUTTER, NATHANIEL ("Staple of News"), a compiler of general news. (See Cunningham).

BUTTERY-HATCH, half-door shutting off the buttery, where provisions and liquors were stored.

BUY, "he bought me," formerly the guardianship of wards could be bought.

BUZ, exclamation to enjoin silence.

BUZZARD, simpleton.

BY AND BY, at once.

BY(E), "on the ___," incidentally, as of minor or secondary importance; at the side.

BY-CHOP, by-blow, bastard.

CADUCEUS, Mercury's wand.

CALIVER, light kind of musket.

CALLET, woman of ill repute.

CALLOT, coif worn on the wigs of our judges or serjeants-at-law (Gifford).

CALVERED, crimped, or sliced and pickled. (See Nares).

CAMOUCCIO, wretch, knave.

CAMUSED, flat.

CAN, knows.

CANDLE-RENT, rent from house property.

CANDLE-WASTER, one who studies late.

CANTER, sturdy beggar.

CAP OF MAINTENCE, an insignia of dignity, a cap of state borne before kings at their coronation; also an heraldic term.

CAPABLE, able to comprehend, fit to receive instruction, impression.

CAPANEUS, one of the "Seven against Thebes."

CARACT, carat, unit of weight for precious stones, etc.; value, worth.

CARANZA, Spanish author of a book on duelling.

CARCANET, jewelled ornament for the neck.

CARE, take care; object.

CAROSH, coach, carriage.

CARPET, table-cover.

CARRIAGE, bearing, behaviour.

CARWHITCHET, quip, pun.

CASAMATE, casemate, fortress.

CASE, a pair.

CASE, "in —," in condition.

CASSOCK, soldier's loose overcoat.

CAST, flight of hawks, couple.

CAST, throw dice; vomit; forecast, calculate.

CAST, cashiered.

CASTING-GLASS, bottle for sprinkling perfume.

CASTRIL, kestrel, falcon.

CAT, structure used in sieges.

CATAMITE, old form of "ganymede."

CATASTROPHE, conclusion.

CATCHPOLE, sheriff's officer.

CATES, dainties, provisions.

CATSO, rogue, cheat.

CAUTELOUS, crafty, artful.

CENSURE, criticism; sentence.

CENSURE, criticise; pass sentence, doom.

CERUSE, cosmetic containing white lead.

CESS, assess.

CHANGE, "hunt —," follow a fresh scent.

CHAPMAN, retail dealer.

CHARACTER, handwriting.

CHARGE, expense.

CHARM, subdue with magic, lay a spell on, silence.

CHARMING, exercising magic power.

CHARTEL, challenge.

CHEAP, bargain, market.

CHEAR, CHEER, comfort, encouragement; food, entertainment.

CHECK AT, aim reproof at.

CHEQUIN, gold Italian coin.

133

CHEVRIL, from kidskin, which is elastic and pliable.

CHIAUS, Turkish envoy; used for a cheat, swindler.

CHILDERMASS DAY, Innocents' Day.

CHOKE-BAIL, action which does not allow of bail.

CHRYSOPOEIA, alchemy.

CHRYSOSPERM, ways of producing gold.

CIBATION, adding fresh substances to supply the waste of evaporation.

CIMICI, bugs.

CINOPER, cinnabar.

CIOPPINI, chopine, lady's high shoe.

CIRCLING BOY, "a species of roarer; one who in some way drew a man into a snare, to cheat or rob him" (Nares).

CIRCUMSTANCE, circumlocution, beating about the bush; ceremony, everything pertaining to a certain condition; detail, particular.

CITRONISE, turn citron colour.

CITTERN, kind of guitar.

CITY-WIRES, woman of fashion, who made use of wires for hair and dress.

CIVIL, legal.

CLAP, clack, chatter.

CLAPPER-DUDGEON, downright beggar.

CLAPS HIS DISH, a clap, or clack, dish (dish with a movable lid) was carried by beggars and lepers to show that the vessel was empty, and to give sound of their approach.

CLARIDIANA, heroine of an old romance.

CLARISSIMO, Venetian noble.

CLEM, starve.

CLICKET, latch.

CLIM O' THE CLOUGHS, etc., wordy heroes of romance.

CLIMATE, country.

CLOSE, secret, private; secretive.

CLOSENESS, secrecy.

CLOTH, arras, hangings.

CLOUT, mark shot at, bull's eye.

CLOWN, countryman, clodhopper.

COACH-LEAVES, folding blinds.

COALS, "bear no —," submit to no affront.

COAT-ARMOUR, coat of arms.

COAT-CARD, court-card.

COB-HERRING, HERRING-COB, a young herring.

COB-SWAN, male swan.

COCK-A-HOOP, denoting unstinted jollity; thought to be derived from turning on the tap that all might drink to the full of the flowing liquor.

COCKATRICE, reptile supposed to be produced from a cock's egg and to kill by its eye — used as a term of reproach for a woman.

COCK-BRAINED, giddy, wild.

COCKER, pamper.

135

COCKSCOMB, fool's cap.

COCKSTONE, stone said to be found in a cock's gizzard, and to possess particular virtues.

CODLING, softening by boiling.

COFFIN, raised crust of a pie.

COG, cheat, wheedle.

COIL, turmoil, confusion, ado.

COKELY, master of a puppet-show (Whalley).

COKES, fool, gull.

COLD-CONCEITED, having cold opinion of, coldly affected towards.

COLE-HARBOUR, a retreat for people of all sorts.

COLLECTION, composure; deduction.

COLLOP, small slice, piece of flesh.

COLLY, blacken.

COLOUR, pretext.

COLOURS, "fear no —," no enemy (quibble).

COLSTAFF, cowlstaff, pole for carrying a cowl=tub.

COME ABOUT, charge, turn round.

COMFORTABLE BREAD, spiced gingerbread.

COMING, forward, ready to respond, complaisant.

COMMENT, commentary; "sometime it is taken for a lie or fayned tale" (Bullokar, 1616).

COMMODITY, "current for —," allusion to practice of moneylenders, who forced the borrower to take part of the loan in the shape of worthless goods on which the latter had to make money if he could.

COMMUNICATE, share.

COMPASS, "in —," within the range, sphere.

COMPLEMENT, completion, completement; anything required for the perfecting or carrying out of a person or affair; accomplishment.

COMPLEXION, natural disposition, constitution.

COMPLIMENT, See Complement.

COMPLIMENTARIES, masters of accomplishments.

COMPOSITION, constitution; agreement, contract.

COMPOSURE, composition.

COMPTER, COUNTER, debtors' prison.

CONCEALMENT, a certain amount of church property had been retained at the dissolution of the monasteries; Elizabeth sent commissioners to search it out, and the courtiers begged for it.

CONCEIT, idea, fancy, witty invention, conception, opinion.

CONCEIT, apprehend.

CONCEITED, fancifully, ingeniously devised or conceived; possessed of intelligence, witty, ingenious (hence well conceited, etc.); disposed to joke; of opinion, possessed of an idea.

CONCEIVE, understand.

CONCENT, harmony, agreement.

CONCLUDE, infer, prove.

CONCOCT, assimilate, digest.

CONDEN'T, probably conducted.

CONDUCT, escort, conductor.

CONEY-CATCH, cheat.

CONFECT, sweetmeat.

CONFER, compare.

CONGIES, bows.

CONNIVE, give a look, wink, of secret intelligence.

CONSORT, company, concert.

CONSTANCY, fidelity, ardour, persistence.

CONSTANT, confirmed, persistent, faithful.

CONSTANTLY, firmly, persistently.

CONTEND, strive.

CONTINENT, holding together.

CONTROL (the point), bear or beat down.

CONVENT, assembly, meeting.

CONVERT, turn (oneself).

CONVEY, transmit from one to another.

CONVINCE, evince, prove; overcome, overpower; convict.
COP, head, top; tuft on head of birds; "a cop" may have reference to one or other meaning; Gifford and others interpret as "conical, terminating in a point."

COPE-MAN, chapman.

COPESMATE, companion.

COPY (Lat. copia), abundance, copiousness.

CORN ("powder —"), grain.

COROLLARY, finishing part or touch.

CORSIVE, corrosive.

CORTINE, curtain, (arch.) wall between two towers, etc.

CORYAT, famous for his travels, published as "Coryat's Crudities."

COSSET, pet lamb, pet.

COSTARD, head.

COSTARD-MONGER, apple-seller, coster-monger.

COSTS, ribs.

COTE, hut.

COTHURNAL, from "cothurnus," a particular boot worn by actors in Greek tragedy.

COTQUEAN, hussy.

COUNSEL, secret.

COUNTENANCE, means necessary for support; credit, standing.

COUNTER. See Compter.

COUNTER, pieces of metal or ivory for calculating at play.

COUNTER, "hunt —," follow scent in reverse direction.

COUNTERFEIT, false coin.

COUNTERPANE, one part or counterpart of a deed or indenture.

COUNTERPOINT, opposite, contrary point.

COURT-DISH, a kind of drinking-cup (Halliwell); N.E.D. quotes from Bp. Goodman's "Court of James I.": "The king...caused his carver to cut him out a court-dish, that is, something of every dish, which he sent him as part of his reversion," but this does not sound like short allowance or small receptacle.

COURT-DOR, fool.

COURTEAU, curtal, small horse with docked tail.

COURTSHIP, courtliness.

COVETISE, avarice.

COWSHARD, cow dung.

COXCOMB, fool's cap, fool.

COY, shrink; disdain.

COYSTREL, low varlet.

COZEN, cheat.

CRACK, lively young rogue, wag.

CRACK, crack up, boast; come to grief.

CRAMBE, game of crambo, in which the players find rhymes for a given word.

CRANCH, craunch.

CRANION, spider-like; also fairy appellation for a fly (Gifford, who refers to lines in Drayton's "Nimphidia").

CRIMP, game at cards.

CRINCLE, draw back, turn aside.

CRISPED, with curled or waved hair.

CROP, gather, reap.

CROPSHIRE, a kind of herring. (See N.E.D.)

CROSS, any piece of money, many coins being stamped with a cross.

CROSS AND PILE, heads and tails.

CROSSLET, crucible.

CROWD, fiddle.

CRUDITIES, undigested matter.

CRUMP, curl up.

CRUSADO, Portuguese gold coin, marked with a cross.

CRY ("he that cried Italian"), "speak in a musical cadence," intone, or declaim (?); cry up.

CUCKING-STOOL, used for the ducking of scolds, etc.

CUCURBITE, a gourd-shaped vessel used for distillation.

CUERPO, "in —," in undress.

CULLICE, broth.

CULLION, base fellow, coward.

CULLISEN, badge worn on their arm by servants.

CULVERIN, kind of cannon.

CUNNING, skill.

CUNNING, skilful.

CUNNING-MAN, fortune-teller.

CURE, care for.

CURIOUS(LY), scrupulous, particular; elaborate, elegant(ly), dainty(ly) (hence "in curious").

CURST, shrewish, mischievous.

CURTAL, dog with docked tail, of inferior sort.

CUSTARD, "quaking —," " — politic," reference to a large custard which formed part of a city feast and afforded huge entertainment, for the fool jumped into it, and other like tricks were played. (See "All's Well, etc." ii. 5, 40.)

CUTWORK, embroidery, open-work.

CYPRES (CYPRUS) (quibble), cypress (or cyprus) being a transparent material, and when black used for mourning.

DAGGER (" — frumety"), name of tavern.

DARGISON, apparently some person known in ballad or tale.

DAUPHIN MY BOY, refrain of old comic song.

DAW, daunt.

DEAD LIFT, desperate emergency.

DEAR, applied to that which in any way touches us nearly.

DECLINE, turn off from; turn away, aside.

DEFALK, deduct, abate.

DEFEND, forbid.

DEGENEROUS, degenerate.

DEGREES, steps.

DELATE, accuse.

DEMI-CULVERIN, cannon carrying a ball of about ten pounds.

DENIER, the smallest possible coin, being the twelfth part of a sou.

DEPART, part with.

DEPENDANCE, ground of quarrel in duello language.

142

DESERT, reward.

DESIGNMENT, design.

DESPERATE, rash, reckless.

DETECT, allow to be detected, betray, inform against.

DETERMINE, terminate.

DETRACT, draw back, refuse.

DEVICE, masque, show; a thing moved by wires, etc., puppet.

DEVISE, exact in every particular.

DEVISED, invented.

DIAPASM, powdered aromatic herbs, made into balls of perfumed paste. (See Pomander.)

DIBBLE, (?) moustache (N.E.D.); (?) dagger (Cunningham).

DIFFUSED, disordered, scattered, irregular.

DIGHT, dressed.

DILDO, refrain of popular songs; vague term of low meaning.

DIMBLE, dingle, ravine.

DIMENSUM, stated allowance.

DISBASE, debase.

DISCERN, distinguish, show a difference between.

DISCHARGE, settle for.

DISCIPLINE, reformation; ecclesiastical system.

DISCLAIM, renounce all part in.

DISCOURSE, process of reasoning, reasoning faculty.

DISCOURTSHIP, discourtesy.

DISCOVER, betray, reveal; display.

DISFAVOUR, disfigure.

DISPARAGEMENT, legal term applied to the unfitness in any way of a marriage arranged for in the case of wards.

DISPENSE WITH, grant dispensation for.

DISPLAY, extend.

DIS'PLE, discipline, teach by the whip.

DISPOSED, inclined to merriment.

DISPOSURE, disposal.

DISPRISE, depreciate.

DISPUNCT, not punctilious.

DISQUISITION, search.

DISSOLVED, enervated by grief.

DISTANCE, (?) proper measure.

DISTASTE, offence, cause of offence.

DISTASTE, render distasteful.

DISTEMPERED, upset, out of humour.

DIVISION (mus.), variation, modulation.

DOG-BOLT, term of contempt.

DOLE, given in dole, charity.

DOLE OF FACES, distribution of grimaces.

DOOM, verdict, sentence.

DOP, dip, low bow.

DOR, beetle, buzzing insect, drone, idler.

DOR, (?) buzz; "give the —," make a fool of.

DOSSER, pannier, basket.

DOTES, endowments, qualities.

DOTTEREL, plover; gull, fool.

DOUBLE, behave deceitfully.

DOXY, wench, mistress.

DRACHM, Greek silver coin.

DRESS, groom, curry.

DRESSING, coiffure.

DRIFT, intention.

DRYFOOT, track by mere scent of foot.

DUCKING, punishment for minor offences.

DUILL, grieve.

DUMPS, melancholy, originally a mournful melody.

DURINDANA, Orlando's sword.

DWINDLE, shrink away, be overawed.

EAN, yean, bring forth young.

EASINESS, readiness.

EBOLITION, ebullition.

EDGE, sword.

EECH, eke.

EGREGIOUS, eminently excellent.

EKE, also, moreover.

E-LA, highest note in the scale.

EGGS ON THE SPIT, important business on hand.

ELF-LOCK, tangled hair, supposed to be the work of elves.

EMMET, ant.

ENGAGE, involve.

ENGHLE. See Ingle.

ENGHLE, cajole; fondle.

ENGIN(E), device, contrivance; agent; ingenuity, wit.

ENGINER, engineer, deviser, plotter.

ENGINOUS, crafty, full of devices; witty, ingenious.

ENGROSS, monopolise.

ENS, an existing thing, a substance.

ENSIGNS, tokens, wounds.

ENSURE, assure.

ENTERTAIN, take into service.

ENTREAT, plead.

ENTREATY, entertainment.

ENTRY, place where a deer has lately passed.

ENVOY, denouement, conclusion.

ENVY, spite, calumny, dislike, odium.

EPHEMERIDES, calendars.

EQUAL, just, impartial.

ERECTION, elevation in esteem.

ERINGO, candied root of the sea-holly, formerly used as a sweetmeat and aphrodisiac.

ERRANT, arrant.

ESSENTIATE, become assimilated.

ESTIMATION, esteem.

ESTRICH, ostrich.

ETHNIC, heathen.

EURIPUS, flux and reflux.

EVEN, just equable.

EVENT, fate, issue.

EVENT(ED), issue(d).

EVERT, overturn.

EXACUATE, sharpen.

EXAMPLESS, without example or parallel.

EXCALIBUR, King Arthur's sword.

EXEMPLIFY, make an example of.

EXEMPT, separate, exclude.

EXEQUIES, obsequies.

147

EXHALE, drag out.

EXHIBITION, allowance for keep, pocket-money.

EXORBITANT, exceeding limits of propriety or law, inordinate.

EXORNATION, ornament.

EXPECT, wait.

EXPIATE, terminate.

EXPLICATE, explain, unfold.

EXTEMPORAL, extempore, unpremeditated.

EXTRACTION, essence.

EXTRAORDINARY, employed for a special or temporary purpose.

EXTRUDE, expel.

EYE, "in —," in view.

EYEBRIGHT, (?) a malt liquor in which the herb of this name was infused, or a person who sold the same (Gifford).

EYE-TINGE, least shade or gleam.

FACE, appearance.

FACES ABOUT, military word of command.

FACINOROUS, extremely wicked.

FACKINGS, faith.

FACT, deed, act, crime.

FACTIOUS, seditious, belonging to a party, given to party feeling.

FAECES, dregs.

FAGIOLI, French beans.

FAIN, forced, necessitated.

FAITHFUL, believing.

FALL, ruff or band turned back on the shoulders; or, veil.

FALSIFY, feign (fencing term).

FAME, report.

FAMILIAR, attendant spirit.

FANTASTICAL, capricious, whimsical.

FARCE, stuff.

FAR-FET. See Fet.

FARTHINGAL, hooped petticoat.

FAUCET, tapster.

FAULT, lack; loss, break in line of scent; "for —," in default of.

FAUTOR, partisan.

FAYLES, old table game similar to backgammon.

FEAR(ED), affright(ed).

FEAT, activity, operation; deed, action.

FEAT, elegant, trim.

FEE, "in —" by feudal obligation.

FEIZE, beat, belabour.

FELLOW, term of contempt.

FENNEL, emblem of flattery.

FERE, companion, fellow.

149

FERN-SEED, supposed to have power of rendering invisible.

FET, fetched.

FETCH, trick.

FEUTERER (Fr. vautrier), dog-keeper.

FEWMETS, dung.

FICO, fig.

FIGGUM, (?) jugglery.

FIGMENT, fiction, invention.

FIRK, frisk, move suddenly, or in jerks; "— up," stir up, rouse; "firks mad," suddenly behaves like a madman.

FIT, pay one out, punish.

FITNESS, readiness.

FITTON (FITTEN), lie, invention.

FIVE-AND-FIFTY, "highest number to stand on at primero" (Gifford).

FLAG, to fly low and waveringly.

FLAGON CHAIN, for hanging a smelling-bottle (Fr. flacon) round the neck (?). (See N.E.D.).

FLAP-DRAGON, game similar to snap-dragon.

FLASKET, some kind of basket.

FLAW, sudden gust or squall of wind.

FLAWN, custard.

FLEA, catch fleas.

FLEER, sneer, laugh derisively.

150

FLESH, feed a hawk or dog with flesh to incite it to the chase; initiate in blood-shed; satiate.

FLICKER-MOUSE, bat.

FLIGHT, light arrow.

FLITTER-MOUSE, bat.

FLOUT, mock, speak and act contemptuously.

FLOWERS, pulverised substance.

FLY, familiar spirit.

FOIL, weapon used in fencing; that which sets anything off to advantage.

FOIST, cut-purse, sharper.

FOND(LY), foolish(ly).

FOOT-CLOTH, housings of ornamental cloth which hung down on either side a horse to the ground.

FOOTING, foothold; footstep; dancing.

FOPPERY, foolery.

FOR, "— failing," for fear of failing.

FORBEAR, bear with; abstain from.

FORCE, "hunt at —," run the game down with dogs.

FOREHEAD, modesty; face, assurance, effrontery.

FORESLOW, delay.

FORESPEAK, bewitch; foretell.

FORETOP, front lock of hair which fashion required to be worn upright.

FORGED, fabricated.

FORM, state formally.

FORMAL, shapely; normal; conventional.

FORTHCOMING, produced when required.

FOUNDER, disable with over-riding.

FOURM, form, lair.

FOX, sword.

FRAIL, rush basket in which figs or raisins were packed.

FRAMPULL, peevish, sour-tempered.

FRAPLER, blusterer, wrangler.

FRAYING, "a stag is said to fray his head when he rubs it against a tree to...cause the outward coat of the new horns to fall off" (Gifford).

FREIGHT (of the gazetti), burden (of the newspapers).

FREQUENT, full.

FRICACE, rubbing.

FRICATRICE, woman of low character.

FRIPPERY, old clothes shop.

FROCK, smock-frock.

FROLICS, (?) humorous verses circulated at a feast (N.E.D.); couplets wrapped round sweetmeats (Cunningham).

FRONTLESS, shameless.

FROTED, rubbed.

FRUMETY, hulled wheat boiled in milk and spiced.

FRUMP, flout, sneer.

FUCUS, dye.

FUGEAND, (?) figent: fidgety, restless (N.E.D.).

FULLAM, false dice.

FULMART, polecat.

FULSOME, foul, offensive.

FURIBUND, raging, furious.

GALLEY-FOIST, city-barge, used on Lord Mayor's Day, when he was sworn into his office at Westminster (Whalley).

GALLIARD, lively dance in triple time.

GAPE, be eager after.

GARAGANTUA, Rabelais' giant.

GARB, sheaf (Fr. gerbe); manner, fashion, behaviour.

GARD, guard, trimming, gold or silver lace, or other ornament.

GARDED, faced or trimmed.

GARNISH, fee.

GAVEL-KIND, name of a land-tenure existing chiefly in Kent; from 16th century often used to denote custom of dividing a deceased man's property equally among his sons (N.E.D.).

GAZETTE, small Venetian coin worth about three-farthings.

GEANCE, jaunt, errand.

GEAR (GEER), stuff, matter, affair.

GELID, frozen.

GEMONIES, steps from which the bodies of criminals were thrown into the river.

GENERAL, free, affable.

GENIUS, attendant spirit.

GENTRY, gentlemen; manners characteristic of gentry, good breeding.

GIB-CAT, tom-cat.

GIGANTOMACHIZE, start a giants' war.

GIGLOT, wanton.

GIMBLET, gimlet.

GING, gang.

GLASS ("taking in of shadows, etc."), crystal or beryl.

GLEEK, card game played by three; party of three, trio; side glance.

GLICK (GLEEK), jest, gibe.

GLIDDER, glaze.

GLORIOUSLY, of vain glory.

GODWIT, bird of the snipe family.

GOLD-END-MAN, a buyer of broken gold and silver.

GOLL, hand.

GONFALIONIER, standard-bearer, chief magistrate, etc.

GOOD, sound in credit.

GOOD-YEAR, good luck.

GOOSE-TURD, colour of. (See Turd).

GORCROW, carrion crow.

GORGET, neck armour.

GOSSIP, godfather.

GOWKED, from "gowk," to stand staring and gaping like a fool.

GRANNAM, grandam.

GRASS, (?) grease, fat.

GRATEFUL, agreeable, welcome.

GRATIFY, give thanks to.

GRATITUDE, gratuity.

GRATULATE, welcome, congratulate.

GRAVITY, dignity.

GRAY, badger.

GRICE, cub.

GRIEF, grievance.

GRIPE, vulture, griffin.

GRIPE'S EGG, vessel in shape of.

GROAT, fourpence.

GROGRAN, coarse stuff made of silk and mohair, or of coarse silk.

GROOM-PORTER, officer in the royal household.

GROPE, handle, probe.

GROUND, pit (hence "grounded judgments").

GUARD, caution, heed.

GUARDANT, heraldic term: turning the head only.

GUILDER, Dutch coin worth about 4d.

GULES, gullet, throat; heraldic term for red.

GULL, simpleton, dupe.

GUST, taste.

HAB NAB, by, on, chance.

HABERGEON, coat of mail.

HAGGARD, wild female hawk; hence coy, wild.

HALBERD, combination of lance and battle-axe.

HALL, "a —!" a cry to clear the room for the dancers.

HANDSEL, first money taken.

HANGER, loop or strap on a sword-belt from which the sword was suspended.

HAP, fortune, luck.

HAPPILY, haply.

HAPPINESS, appropriateness, fitness.

HAPPY, rich.

HARBOUR, track, trace (an animal) to its shelter.

HARD-FAVOURED, harsh-featured.

HARPOCRATES, Horus the child, son of Osiris, figured with a finger pointing to his mouth, indicative of silence.

HARRINGTON, a patent was granted to Lord H. for the coinage of tokens (q.v.).

HARROT, herald.

HARRY NICHOLAS, founder of a community called the "Family of Love."

HAY, net for catching rabbits, etc.

HAY! (Ital. hai!), you have it (a fencing term).

HAY IN HIS HORN, ill-tempered person.

HAZARD, game at dice; that which is staked.

HEAD, "first —," young deer with antlers first sprouting; fig. a newly-ennobled man.

HEADBOROUGH, constable.

HEARKEN AFTER, inquire; "hearken out," find, search out.

HEARTEN, encourage.

HEAVEN AND HELL ("Alchemist"), names of taverns.

HECTIC, fever.

HEDGE IN, include.

HELM, upper part of a retort.

HER'NSEW, hernshaw, heron.

HIERONIMO (JERONIMO), hero of Kyd's "Spanish Tragedy."

HOBBY, nag.

HOBBY-HORSE, imitation horse of some light material, fastened round the waist of the morrice-dancer, who imitated the movements of a skittish horse.

HODDY-DODDY, fool.

HOIDEN, hoyden, formerly applied to both sexes (ancient term for leveret? Gifford).

HOLLAND, name of two famous chemists.

HONE AND HONERO, wailing expressions of lament or discontent.

HOOD-WINK'D, blindfolded.

HORARY, hourly.

HORN-MAD, stark mad (quibble).

HORN-THUMB, cut-purses were in the habit of wearing a horn shield on the thumb.

HORSE-BREAD-EATING, horses were often fed on coarse bread.

HORSE-COURSER, horse-dealer.

HOSPITAL, Christ's Hospital.

HOWLEGLAS, Eulenspiegel, the hero of a popular German tale which relates his buffooneries and knavish tricks.

HUFF, hectoring, arrogance.

HUFF IT, swagger.

HUISHER (Fr. huissier), usher.

HUM, beer and spirits mixed together.

HUMANITIAN, humanist, scholar.

HUMOROUS, capricious, moody, out of humour; moist.

HUMOUR, a word used in and out of season in the time of Shakespeare and Ben Jonson, and ridiculed by both.

HUMOURS, manners.

HUMPHREY, DUKE, those who were dinnerless spent the dinner-hour in a part of St. Paul's where stood a monument said to be that of the duke's; hence "dine with Duke Humphrey," to go hungry.

HURTLESS, harmless.

IDLE, useless, unprofitable.

ILL-AFFECTED, ill-disposed.

ILL-HABITED, unhealthy.

ILLUSTRATE, illuminate.

IMBIBITION, saturation, steeping.

IMBROCATA, fencing term: a thrust in tierce.

IMPAIR, impairment.

IMPART, give money.

IMPARTER, any one ready to be cheated and to part with his money.

IMPEACH, damage.

IMPERTINENCIES, irrelevancies.

IMPERTINENT(LY), irrelevant(ly), without reason or purpose.

IMPOSITION, duty imposed by.

IMPOTENTLY, beyond power of control.

IMPRESS, money in advance.

IMPULSION, incitement.

IN AND IN, a game played by two or three persons with four dice.

INCENSE, incite, stir up.

INCERATION, act of covering with wax; or reducing a substance to softness of wax.

INCH, "to their —es," according to their stature, capabilities.

INCH-PIN, sweet-bread.

INCONVENIENCE, inconsistency, absurdity.

INCONY, delicate, rare (used as a term of affection).

INCUBEE, incubus.

INCUBUS, evil spirit that oppresses us in sleep, nightmare.

INCURIOUS, unfastidious, uncritical.

INDENT, enter into engagement.

INDIFFERENT, tolerable, passable.

INDIGESTED, shapeless, chaotic.

INDUCE, introduce.

INDUE, supply.

INEXORABLE, relentless.

INFANTED, born, produced.

INFLAME, augment charge.

INGENIOUS, used indiscriminantly for ingenuous; intelligent, talented.

INGENUITY, ingenuousness.

INGENUOUS, generous.

INGINE. See Engin.

INGINER, engineer. (See Enginer).

INGLE, OR ENGHLE, bosom friend, intimate, minion.

INHABITABLE, uninhabitable.

INJURY, insult, affront.

IN-MATE, resident, indwelling.

INNATE, natural.

INNOCENT, simpleton.

INQUEST, jury, or other official body of inquiry.

INQUISITION, inquiry.

INSTANT, immediate.

INSTRUMENT, legal document.

INSURE, assure.

INTEGRATE, complete, perfect.

INTELLIGENCE, secret information, news.

INTEND, note carefully, attend, give ear to, be occupied with.

INTENDMENT, intention.

INTENT, intention, wish.

INTENTION, concentration of attention or gaze.

INTENTIVE, attentive.

INTERESSED, implicated.

INTRUDE, bring in forcibly or without leave.

INVINCIBLY, invisibly.

INWARD, intimate.

IRPE (uncertain), "a fantastic grimace, or contortion of the body: (Gifford).

JACK, Jack o' the clock, automaton figure that strikes the hour; Jack-a-lent, puppet thrown at in Lent.

161

JACK, key of a virginal.

JACOB'S STAFF, an instrument for taking altitudes and distances.

JADE, befool.

JEALOUSY, JEALOUS, suspicion, suspicious.

JERKING, lashing.

JEW'S TRUMP, Jew's harp.

JIG, merry ballad or tune; a fanciful dialogue or light comic act introduced at the end or during an interlude of a play.

JOINED (JOINT)-STOOL, folding stool.

JOLL, jowl.

JOLTHEAD, blockhead.

JUMP, agree, tally.

JUST YEAR, no one was capable of the consulship until he was forty-three.

KELL, cocoon.

KELLY, an alchemist.

KEMB, comb.

KEMIA, vessel for distillation.

KIBE, chap, sore.

KILDERKIN, small barrel.

KILL, kiln.

KIND, nature; species; "do one's —," act according to one's nature.

KIRTLE, woman's gown of jacket and petticoat.

162

KISS OR DRINK AFORE ME, "this is a familiar expression, employed when what the speaker is just about to say is anticipated by another" (Gifford).

KIT, fiddle.

KNACK, snap, click.

KNIPPER-DOLING, a well-known Anabaptist.

KNITTING CUP, marriage cup.

KNOCKING, striking, weighty.

KNOT, company, band; a sandpiper or robin snipe (Tringa canutus); flower-bed laid out in fanciful design.

KURSINED, KYRSIN, christened.

LABOURED, wrought with labour and care.

LADE, load(ed).

LADING, load.

LAID, plotted.

LANCE-KNIGHT (Lanzknecht), a German mercenary foot-soldier.

LAP, fold.

LAR, household god.

LARD, garnish.

LARGE, abundant.

LARUM, alarum, call to arms.

LATTICE, tavern windows were furnished with lattices of various colours.

LAUNDER, to wash gold in aqua regia, so as imperceptibly to extract some of it.

LAVE, ladle, bale.

LAW, "give —," give a start (term of chase).

LAXATIVE, loose.

LAY ABOARD, run alongside generally with intent to board.

LEAGUER, siege, or camp of besieging army.

LEASING, lying.

LEAVE, leave off, desist.

LEER, leering or "empty, hence, perhaps, leer horse, a horse without a rider; leer is an adjective meaning uncontrolled, hence 'leer drunkards'" (Halliwell); according to Nares, a leer (empty) horse meant also a led horse; leeward, left.

LEESE, lose.

LEGS, "make —," do obeisance.

LEIGER, resident representative.

LEIGERITY, legerdemain.

LEMMA, subject proposed, or title of the epigram.

LENTER, slower.

LET, hinder.

LET, hindrance.

LEVEL COIL, a rough game...in which one hunted another from his seat. Hence used for any noisy riot (Halliwell).

LEWD, ignorant.

LEYSTALLS, receptacles of filth.

LIBERAL, ample.

LIEGER, ledger, register.

LIFT(ING), steal(ing); theft.

LIGHT, alight.

LIGHTLY, commonly, usually, often.

LIKE, please.

LIKELY, agreeable, pleasing.

LIME-HOUND, leash-, blood-hound.

LIMMER, vile, worthless.

LIN, leave off.

Line, "by —," by rule.

LINSTOCK, staff to stick in the ground, with forked head to hold a lighted match for firing cannon.

LIQUID, clear.

LIST, listen, hark; like, please.

LIVERY, legal term, delivery of the possession, etc.

LOGGET, small log, stick.

LOOSE, solution; upshot, issue; release of an arrow.

LOSE, give over, desist from; waste.

LOUTING, bowing, cringing.

LUCULENT, bright of beauty.

LUDGATHIANS, dealers on Ludgate Hill.

LURCH, rob, cheat.

LUTE, to close a vessel with some kind of cement.

MACK, unmeaning expletive.

MADGE-HOWLET or OWL, barn-owl.

MAIM, hurt, injury.

MAIN, chief concern (used as a quibble on heraldic term for "hand").

MAINPRISE, becoming surety for a prisoner so as to procure his release.

MAINTENANCE, giving aid, or abetting.

MAKE, mate.

MAKE, MADE, acquaint with business, prepare(d), instruct(ed).

MALLANDERS, disease of horses.

MALT HORSE, dray horse.

MAMMET, puppet.

MAMMOTHREPT, spoiled child.

MANAGE, control (term used for breaking-in horses); handling, administration.

MANGO, slave-dealer.

MANGONISE, polish up for sale.

MANIPLES, bundles, handfuls.

MANKIND, masculine, like a virago.

MANKIND, humanity.

MAPLE FACE, spotted face (N.E.D.).

MARCHPANE, a confection of almonds, sugar, etc.

MARK, "fly to the —," "generally said of a goshawk when, having 'put in' a covey of partridges, she takes stand, marking the spot where they disappeared from view until the falconer arrives to put them out to her" (Harting, Bibl. Accip. Gloss. 226).

MARLE, marvel.

MARROW-BONE MAN, one often on his knees for prayer.

MARRY! exclamation derived from the Virgin's name.

MARRY GIP, "probably originated from By Mary Gipcy = St. Mary of Egypt, (N.E.D.).

MARTAGAN, Turk's cap lily.

MARYHINCHCO, stringhalt.

MASORETH, Masora, correct form of the scriptural text according to Hebrew tradition.

MASS, abb. for master.

MAUND, beg.

MAUTHER, girl, maid.

MEAN, moderation.

MEASURE, dance, more especially a stately one.

MEAT, "carry — in one's mouth," be a source of money or entertainment.

MEATH, metheglin.

MECHANICAL, belonging to mechanics, mean, vulgar.

MEDITERRANEO, middle aisle of St. Paul's, a general resort for business and amusement.

MEET WITH, even with.

MELICOTTON, a late kind of peach.

MENSTRUE, solvent.

MERCAT, market.

MERD, excrement.

MERE, undiluted; absolute, unmitigated.

MESS, party of four.

METHEGLIN, fermented liquor, of which one ingredient was honey.

METOPOSCOPY, study of physiognomy.

MIDDLING GOSSIP, go-between.

MIGNIARD, dainty, delicate.

MILE-END, training-ground of the city.

MINE-MEN, sappers.

MINION, form of cannon.

MINSITIVE, (?) mincing, affected (N.E.D.).

MISCELLANY MADAM, "a female trader in miscellaneous articles; a dealer in trinkets or ornaments of various kinds, such as kept shops in the New Exchange" (Nares).

MISCELLINE, mixed grain; medley.

MISCONCEIT, misconception.

MISPRISE, MISPRISION, mistake, misunderstanding.

MISTAKE AWAY, carry away as if by mistake.

MITHRIDATE, an antidote against poison.

MOCCINIGO, small Venetian coin, worth about ninepence.

MODERN, in the mode; ordinary, commonplace.

168

MOMENT, force or influence of value.

MONTANTO, upward stroke.

MONTH'S MIND, violent desire.

MOORISH, like a moor or waste.

MORGLAY, sword of Bevis of Southampton.

MORRICE-DANCE, dance on May Day, etc., in which certain personages were represented.

MORTALITY, death.

MORT-MAL, old sore, gangrene.

MOSCADINO, confection flavoured with musk.

MOTHER, Hysterica passio.

MOTION, proposal, request; puppet, puppet-show; "one of the small figures on the face of a large clock which was moved by the vibration of the pendulum" (Whalley).

MOTION, suggest, propose.

MOTLEY, parti-coloured dress of a fool; hence used to signify pertaining to, or like, a fool.

MOTTE, motto.

MOURNIVAL, set of four aces or court cards in a hand; a quartette.

MOW, setord hay or sheaves of grain.

MUCH! expressive of irony and incredulity.

MUCKINDER, handkerchief.

MULE, "born to ride on —," judges or serjeants-at-law formerly rode on mules when going in state to Westminster (Whally).

MULLETS, small pincers.

MUM-CHANCE, game of chance, played in silence.

MUN, must.

MUREY, dark crimson red.

MUSCOVY-GLASS, mica.

MUSE, wonder.

MUSICAL, in harmony.

MUSS, mouse; scramble.

MYROBOLANE, foreign conserve, "a dried plum, brought
from the Indies."

MYSTERY, art, trade, profession.

NAIL, "to the —" (ad unguem), to perfection, to the
very utmost.

NATIVE, natural.

NEAT, cattle.

NEAT, smartly apparelled; unmixed; dainty.

NEATLY, neatly finished.

NEATNESS, elegance.

NEIS, nose, scent.

NEUF (NEAF, NEIF), fist.

NEUFT, newt.

NIAISE, foolish, inexperienced person.

NICE, fastidious, trivial, finical, scrupulous.

NICENESS, fastidiousness.

NICK, exact amount; right moment; "set in the —," meaning uncertain.

NICE, suit, fit; hit, seize the right moment, etc., exactly hit on, hit off.

NOBLE, gold coin worth 6s. 8d.

NOCENT, harmful.

NIL, not will.

NOISE, company of musicians.

NOMENTACK, an Indian chief from Virginia.

NONES, nonce.

NOTABLE, egregious.

NOTE, sign, token.

NOUGHT, "be —," go to the devil, be hanged, etc.

NOWT-HEAD, blockhead.

NUMBER, rhythm.

NUPSON, oaf, simpleton.

OADE, woad.

OBARNI, preparation of mead.

OBJECT, oppose; expose; interpose.

OBLATRANT, barking, railing.

OBNOXIOUS, liable, exposed; offensive.

OBSERVANCE, homage, devoted service.

OBSERVANT, attentive, obsequious.

OBSERVE, show deference, respect.

OBSERVER, one who shows deference, or waits upon another.

OBSTANCY, legal phrase, "juridical opposition."

OBSTREPEROUS, clamorous, vociferous.

OBSTUPEFACT, stupefied.

ODLING, (?) "must have some relation to tricking and cheating" (Nares).

OMINOUS, deadly, fatal.

ONCE, at once; for good and all; used also for additional emphasis.

ONLY, pre-eminent, special.

OPEN, make public; expound.

OPPILATION, obstruction.

OPPONE, oppose.

OPPOSITE, antagonist.

OPPRESS, suppress.

ORIGINOUS, native.

ORT, remnant, scrap.

OUT, "to be —," to have forgotten one's part; not at one with each other.

OUTCRY, sale by auction.

OUTRECUIDANCE, arrogance, presumption.

OUTSPEAK, speak more than.

OVERPARTED, given too difficult a part to play.

OWLSPIEGEL. See Howleglass.

OYEZ! (O YES!), hear ye! call of the public crier when about to make a proclamation.

PACKING PENNY, "give a —," dismiss, send packing.

PAD, highway.

PAD-HORSE, road-horse.

PAINED (PANED) SLOPS, full breeches made of strips of different colour and material.

PAINFUL, diligent, painstaking.

PAINT, blush.

PALINODE, ode of recantation.

PALL, weaken, dim, make stale.

PALM, triumph.

PAN, skirt of dress or coat.

PANNEL, pad, or rough kind of saddle.

PANNIER-ALLY, inhabited by tripe-sellers.

PANNIER-MAN, hawker; a man employed about the inns of court to bring in provisions, set the table, etc.

PANTOFLE, indoor shoe, slipper.

PARAMENTOS, fine trappings.

PARANOMASIE, a play upon words.

PARANTORY, (?) peremptory.

PARCEL, particle, fragment (used contemptuously); article.

173

PARCEL, part, partly.

PARCEL-POET, poetaster.

PARERGA, subordinate matters.

PARGET, to paint or plaster the face.

PARLE, parley.

PARLOUS, clever, shrewd.

PART, apportion.

PARTAKE, participate in.

PARTED, endowed, talented.

PARTICULAR, individual person.

PARTIZAN, kind of halberd.

PARTRICH, partridge.

PARTS, qualities, endowments.

PASH, dash, smash.

PASS, care, trouble oneself.

PASSADO, fencing term: a thrust.

PASSAGE, game at dice.

PASSINGLY, exceedingly.

PASSION, effect caused by external agency.

PASSION, "in —," in so melancholy a tone, so pathetically.

PATOUN, (?) Fr. Paton, pellet of dough; perhaps the "moulding of the tobacco...for the pipe" (Gifford); (?) variant of Petun, South American name of tobacco.

PATRICO, the recorder, priest, orator of strolling beggars or gipsies.

PATTEN, shoe with wooden sole; "go —," keep step with, accompany.

PAUCA VERBA, few words.

PAVIN, a stately dance.

PEACE, "with my master's —," by leave, favour.

PECULIAR, individual, single.

PEDANT, teacher of the languages.

PEEL, baker's shovel.

PEEP, speak in a small or shrill voice.

PEEVISH(LY), foolish(ly), capricious(ly); childish(ly).

PELICAN, a retort fitted with tube or tubes, for continuous distillation.

PENCIL, small tuft of hair.

PERDUE, soldier accustomed to hazardous service.

PEREMPTORY, resolute, bold; imperious; thorough, utter, absolute(ly).

PERIMETER, circumference of a figure.

PERIOD, limit, end.

PERK, perk up.

PERPETUANA, "this seems to be that glossy kind of stuff now called everlasting, and anciently worn by serjeants and other city officers" (Gifford).

PERSPECTIVE, a view, scene or scenery; an optical device which gave a distortion to the picture unless seen from a particular point; a relief, modelled to produce an optical illusion.

PERSPICIL, optic glass.

PERSTRINGE, criticise, censure.

PERSUADE, inculcate, commend.

PERSWAY, mitigate.

PERTINACY, pertinacity.

PESTLING, pounding, pulverising, like a pestle.

PETASUS, broad-brimmed hat or winged cap worn by Mercury.

PETITIONARY, supplicatory.

PETRONEL, a kind of carbine or light gun carried by horsemen.

PETULANT, pert, insolent.

PHERE. See Fere.

PHLEGMA, watery distilled liquor (old chem. "water").

PHRENETIC, madman.

PICARDIL, stiff upright collar fastened on to the coat (Whalley).

PICT-HATCH, disreputable quarter of London.

PIECE, person, used for woman or girl; a gold coin worth in Jonson's time 20s. or 22s.

PIECES OF EIGHT, Spanish coin: piastre equal to eight reals.

PIED, variegated.

PIE-POUDRES (Fr. pied-poudreux, dusty-foot), court held at fairs to administer justice to itinerant vendors and buyers.

PILCHER, term of contempt; one who wore a buff or leather jerkin, as did the serjeants of the counter; a pilferer.

PILED, pilled, peeled, bald.

PILL'D, polled, fleeced.

PIMLICO, "sometimes spoken of as a person — perhaps master of a house famous for a particular ale" (Gifford).

PINE, afflict, distress.

PINK, stab with a weapon; pierce or cut in scallops for ornament.

PINNACE, a go-between in infamous sense.

PISMIRE, ant.

PISTOLET, gold coin, worth about 6s.

PITCH, height of a bird of prey's flight.

PLAGUE, punishment, torment.

PLAIN, lament.

PLAIN SONG, simple melody.

PLAISE, plaice.

PLANET, "struck with a —," planets were supposed to have powers of blasting or exercising secret influences.

PLAUSIBLE, pleasing.

PLAUSIBLY, approvingly.

PLOT, plan.

PLY, apply oneself to.

POESIE, posy, motto inside a ring.

POINT IN HIS DEVICE, exact in every particular.

POINTS, tagged laces or cords for fastening the breeches to the doublet.

POINT-TRUSSER, one who trussed (tied) his master's points (q.v.).

POISE, weigh, balance.

POKING-STICK, stick used for setting the plaits of ruffs.

POLITIC, politician.

POLITIC, judicious, prudent, political.

POLITICIAN, plotter, intriguer.

POLL, strip, plunder, gain by extortion.

POMANDER, ball of perfume, worn or hung about the person to prevent infection, or for foppery.

POMMADO, vaulting on a horse without the aid of stirrups.

PONTIC, sour.

POPULAR, vulgar, of the populace.

POPULOUS, numerous.

PORT, gate; print of a deer's foot.

PORT, transport.

PORTAGUE, Portuguese gold coin, worth over 3 or 4 pounds.

PORTCULLIS, "— of coin," some old coins have a portcullis stamped on their reverse (Whalley).

PORTENT, marvel, prodigy; sinister omen.

PORTENTOUS, prophesying evil, threatening.

PORTER, references appear "to allude to Parsons, the king's porter, who was...near seven feet high" (Whalley).

POSSESS, inform, acquaint.

POST AND PAIR, a game at cards.

POSY, motto. (See Poesie).

POTCH, poach.

POULT-FOOT, club-foot.

POUNCE, claw, talon.

PRACTICE, intrigue, concerted plot.

PRACTISE, plot, conspire.

PRAGMATIC, an expert, agent.

PRAGMATIC, officious, conceited, meddling.

PRECEDENT, record of proceedings.

PRECEPT, warrant, summons.

PRECISIAN(ISM), Puritan(ism), preciseness.

PREFER, recommend.

PRESENCE, presence chamber.

PRESENT(LY), immediate(ly), without delay; at the present time; actually.

PRESS, force into service.

PREST, ready.

PRETEND, assert, allege.

PREVENT, anticipate.

PRICE, worth, excellence.

PRICK, point, dot used in the writing of Hebrew and other languages.

PRICK, prick out, mark off, select; trace, track; "— away," make off with speed.

PRIMERO, game of cards.

PRINCOX, pert boy.

PRINT, "in —," to the letter, exactly.

PRISTINATE, former.

PRIVATE, private interests.

PRIVATE, privy, intimate.

PROCLIVE, prone to.

PRODIGIOUS, monstrous, unnatural.

PRODIGY, monster.

PRODUCED, prolonged.

PROFESS, pretend.

PROJECTION, the throwing of the "powder of projection" into the crucible to turn the melted metal into gold or silver.

PROLATE, pronounce drawlingly.

PROPER, of good appearance, handsome; own, particular.

PROPERTIES, stage necessaries.

PROPERTY, duty; tool.

PRORUMPED, burst out.

PROTEST, vow, proclaim (an affected word of that time);

formally declare non-payment, etc., of bill of exchange; fig. failure of personal credit, etc.

PROVANT, soldier's allowance — hence, of common make.

PROVIDE, foresee.

PROVIDENCE, foresight, prudence.

PUBLICATION, making a thing public of common property (N.E.D.).

PUCKFIST, puff-ball; insipid, insignificant, boasting fellow.

PUFF-WING, shoulder puff.

PUISNE, judge of inferior rank, a junior.

PULCHRITUDE, beauty.

PUMP, shoe.

PUNGENT, piercing.

PUNTO, point, hit.

PURCEPT, precept, warrant.

PURE, fine, capital, excellent.

PURELY, perfectly, utterly.

PURL, pleat or fold of a ruff.

PURSE-NET, net of which the mouth is drawn together with a string.

PURSUIVANT, state messenger who summoned the persecuted seminaries; warrant officer.

PURSY, PURSINESS, shortwinded(ness).

PUT, make a push, exert yourself (N.E.D.).

PUT OFF, excuse, shift.

PUT ON, incite, encourage; proceed with, take in hand, try.

QUACKSALVER, quack.

QUAINT, elegant, elaborated, ingenious, clever.

QUAR, quarry.

QUARRIED, seized, or fed upon, as prey.

QUEAN, hussy, jade.

QUEASY, hazardous, delicate.

QUELL, kill, destroy.

QUEST, request; inquiry.

QUESTION, decision by force of arms.

QUESTMAN, one appointed to make official inquiry.

QUIB, QUIBLIN, quibble, quip.

QUICK, the living.

QUIDDIT, quiddity, legal subtlety.

QUIRK, clever turn or trick.

QUIT, requite, repay; acquit, absolve; rid; forsake, leave.

QUITTER-BONE, disease of horses.

QUODLING, codling.

QUOIT, throw like a quoit, chuck.

QUOTE, take note, observe, write down.

RACK, neck of mutton or pork (Halliwell).

RAKE UP, cover over.

RAMP, rear, as a lion, etc.

RAPT, carry away.

RAPT, enraptured.

RASCAL, young or inferior deer.

RASH, strike with a glancing oblique blow, as a boar with its tusk.

RATSEY, GOMALIEL, a famous highwayman.

RAVEN, devour.

REACH, understand.

REAL, regal.

REBATU, ruff, turned-down collar.

RECTOR, RECTRESS, director, governor.

REDARGUE, confute.

REDUCE, bring back.

REED, rede, counsel, advice.

REEL, run riot.

REFEL, refute.

REFORMADOES, disgraced or disbanded soldiers.

REGIMENT, government.

REGRESSION, return.

REGULAR ("Tale of a Tub"), regular noun (quibble) (N.E.D.).

RELIGION, "make — of," make a point of, scruple of.

RELISH, savour.

REMNANT, scrap of quotation.

REMORA, species of fish.

RENDER, depict, exhibit, show.

REPAIR, reinstate.

REPETITION, recital, narration.

REREMOUSE, bat.

RESIANT, resident.

RESIDENCE, sediment.

RESOLUTION, judgment, decision.

RESOLVE, inform; assure; prepare, make up one's mind; dissolve; come to a decision, be convinced; relax, set at ease.

RESPECTIVE, worthy of respect; regardful, discriminative.

RESPECTIVELY, with reverence.

RESPECTLESS, regardless.

RESPIRE, exhale; inhale.

RESPONSIBLE, correspondent.

REST, musket-rest.

REST, "set up one's —," venture one's all, one's last stake (from game of primero).

REST, arrest.

RESTIVE, RESTY, dull, inactive.

RETCHLESS(NESS), reckless(ness).

RETIRE, cause to retire.

RETRICATO, fencing term.

RETRIEVE, rediscovery of game once sprung.

RETURNS, ventures sent abroad, for the safe return of which so much money is received.

REVERBERATE, dissolve or blend by reflected heat.

REVERSE, REVERSO, back-handed thrust, etc., in fencing.

REVISE, reconsider a sentence.

RHEUM, spleen, caprice.

RIBIBE, abusive term for an old woman.

RID, destroy, do away with.

RIFLING, raffling, dicing.

RING, "cracked within the —," coins so cracked were unfit for currency.

RISSE, risen, rose.

RIVELLED, wrinkled.

ROARER, swaggerer.

ROCHET, fish of the gurnet kind.

ROCK, distaff.

RODOMONTADO, braggadocio.

ROGUE, vagrant, vagabond.

RONDEL, "a round mark in the score of a public-house" (Nares); roundel.

ROOK, sharper; fool, dupe.

ROSAKER, similar to ratsbane.

ROSA-SOLIS, a spiced spirituous liquor.

ROSES, rosettes.

ROUND, "gentlemen of the —," officers of inferior rank.

ROUND TRUNKS, trunk hose, short loose breeches reaching almost or quite to the knees.

ROUSE, carouse, bumper.

ROVER, arrow used for shooting at a random mark at uncertain distance.

ROWLY-POWLY, roly-poly.

RUDE, RUDENESS, unpolished, rough(ness), coarse(ness).

RUFFLE, flaunt, swagger.

RUG, coarse frieze.

RUG-GOWNS, gown made of rug.

RUSH, reference to rushes with which the floors were then strewn.

RUSHER, one who strewed the floor with rushes.

RUSSET, homespun cloth of neutral or reddish-brown colour.

SACK, loose, flowing gown.

SADLY, seriously, with gravity.

SAD(NESS), sober, serious(ness).

SAFFI, bailiffs.

ST. THOMAS A WATERINGS, place in Surrey where criminals were executed.

SAKER, small piece of ordnance.

SALT, leap.

SALT, lascivious.

SAMPSUCHINE, sweet marjoram.

SARABAND, a slow dance.

SATURNALS, began December 17.

SAUCINESS, presumption, insolence.

SAUCY, bold, impudent, wanton.

SAUNA (Lat.), a gesture of contempt.

SAVOUR, perceive; gratify, please; to partake of the nature.

SAY, sample.

SAY, assay, try.

SCALD, word of contempt, implying dirt and disease.

SCALLION, shalot, small onion.

SCANDERBAG, "name which the Turks (in allusion to Alexander the Great) gave to the brave Castriot, chief of Albania, with whom they had continual wars. His romantic life had just been translated" (Gifford).

SCAPE, escape.

SCARAB, beetle.

SCARTOCCIO, fold of paper, cover, cartouch, cartridge.

SCONCE, head.

SCOPE, aim.

SCOT AND LOT, tax, contribution (formerly a parish assessment).

SCOTOMY, dizziness in the head.

SCOUR, purge.

SCOURSE, deal, swap.

SCRATCHES, disease of horses.

SCROYLE, mean, rascally fellow.

SCRUPLE, doubt.

SEAL, put hand to the giving up of property or rights.

SEALED, stamped as genuine.

SEAM-RENT, ragged.

SEAMING LACES, insertion or edging.

SEAR UP, close by searing, burning.

SEARCED, sifted.

SECRETARY, able to keep a secret.

SECULAR, worldly, ordinary, commonplace.

SECURE, confident.

SEELIE, happy, blest.

SEISIN, legal term: possession.

SELLARY, lewd person.

SEMBLABLY, similarly.

SEMINARY, a Romish priest educated in a foreign seminary.

SENSELESS, insensible, without sense or feeling.

SENSIBLY, perceptibly.

SENSIVE, sensitive.

SENSUAL, pertaining to the physical or material.

SERENE, harmful dew of evening.

SERICON, red tincture.

SERVANT, lover.

SERVICES, doughty deeds of arms.

SESTERCE, Roman copper coin.

SET, stake, wager.

SET UP, drill.

SETS, deep plaits of the ruff.

SEWER, officer who served up the feast, and brought water for the hands of the guests.

SHAPE, a suit by way of disguise.

SHIFT, fraud, dodge.

SHIFTER, cheat.

SHITTLE, shuttle; "shittle-cock," shuttlecock.

SHOT, tavern reckoning.

SHOT-CLOG, one only tolerated because he paid the shot (reckoning) for the rest.

SHOT-FREE, scot-free, not having to pay.

SHOVE-GROAT, low kind of gambling amusement, perhaps somewhat of the nature of pitch and toss.

SHOT-SHARKS, drawers.

SHREWD, mischievous, malicious, curst.

189

SHREWDLY, keenly, in a high degree.

SHRIVE, sheriff; posts were set up before his door for proclamations, or to indicate his residence.

SHROVING, Shrovetide, season of merriment.

SIGILLA, seal, mark.

SILENCED BRETHERN, MINISTERS, those of the Church or Nonconformists who had been silenced, deprived, etc.

SILLY, simple, harmless.

SIMPLE, silly, witless; plain, true.

SIMPLES, herbs.

SINGLE, term of chase, signifying when the hunted stag is separated from the herd, or forced to break covert.

SINGLE, weak, silly.

SINGLE-MONEY, small change.

SINGULAR, unique, supreme.

SI-QUIS, bill, advertisement.

SKELDRING, getting money under false pretences; swindling.

SKILL, "it —s not," matters not.

SKINK(ER), pour, draw(er), tapster.

SKIRT, tail.

SLEEK, smooth.

SLICE, fire shovel or pan (dial.).

SLICK, sleek, smooth.

'SLID, 'SLIGHT, 'SPRECIOUS, irreverent oaths.

SLIGHT, sleight, cunning, cleverness; trick.

SLIP, counterfeit coin, bastard.

SLIPPERY, polished and shining.

SLOPS, large loose breeches.

SLOT, print of a stag's foot.

SLUR, put a slur on; cheat (by sliding a die in some way).

SMELT, gull, simpleton.

SNORLE, "perhaps snarl, as Puppy is addressed" (Cunningham).

SNOTTERIE, filth.

SNUFF, anger, resentment; "take in —," take offence at.

SNUFFERS, small open silver dishes for holding snuff, or receptacle for placing snuffers in (Halliwell).

SOCK, shoe worn by comic actors.

SOD, seethe.

SOGGY, soaked, sodden.

SOIL, "take —," said of a hunted stag when he takes to the water for safety.

SOL, sou.

SOLDADOES, soldiers.

SOLICIT, rouse, excite to action.

SOOTH, flattery, cajolery.

SOOTHE, flatter, humour.

SOPHISTICATE, adulterate.

SORT, company, party; rank, degree.

SORT, suit, fit; select.

SOUSE, ear.

SOUSED ("Devil is an Ass"), fol. read "sou't," which Dyce interprets as "a variety of the spelling of "shu'd": to "shu" is to scare a bird away." (See his "Webster," page 350).

SOWTER, cobbler.

SPAGYRICA, chemistry according to the teachings of Paracelsus.

SPAR, bar.

SPEAK, make known, proclaim.

SPECULATION, power of sight.

SPED, to have fared well, prospered.

SPEECE, species.

SPIGHT, anger, rancour.

SPINNER, spider.

SPINSTRY, lewd person.

SPITTLE, hospital, lazar-house.

SPLEEN, considered the seat of the emotions.

SPLEEN, caprice, humour, mood.

SPRUNT, spruce.

SPURGE, foam.

SPUR-RYAL, gold coin worth 15s.

SQUIRE, square, measure; "by the —," exactly.

STAGGERING, wavering, hesitating.

STAIN, disparagement, disgrace.

STALE, decoy, or cover, stalking-horse.

STALE, make cheap, common.

STALK, approach stealthily or under cover.

STALL, forestall.

STANDARD, suit.

STAPLE, market, emporium.

STARK, downright.

STARTING-HOLES, loopholes of escape.

STATE, dignity; canopied chair of state; estate.

STATUMINATE, support vines by poles or stakes; used by Pliny (Gifford).

STAY, gag.

STAY, await; detain.

STICKLER, second or umpire.

STIGMATISE, mark, brand.

STILL, continual(ly), constant(ly).

STINKARD, stinking fellow.

STINT, stop.

STIPTIC, astringent.

STOCCATA, thrust in fencing.

STOCK-FISH, salted and dried fish.

STOMACH, pride, valour.

STOMACH, resent.

STOOP, swoop down as a hawk.

STOP, fill, stuff.

STOPPLE, stopper.

STOTE, stoat, weasel.

STOUP, stoop, swoop=bow.

STRAIGHT, straightway.

STRAMAZOUN (Ital. stramazzone), a down blow, as opposed to the thrust.

STRANGE, like a stranger, unfamiliar.

STRANGENESS, distance of behaviour.

STREIGHTS, OR BERMUDAS, labyrinth of alleys and courts in the Strand.

STRIGONIUM, Grau in Hungary, taken from the Turks in 1597.

STRIKE, balance (accounts).

STRINGHALT, disease of horses.

STROKER, smoother, flatterer.

STROOK, p.p. of "strike."

STRUMMEL-PATCHED, strummel is glossed in dialect dicts as "a long, loose and dishevelled head of hair."

STUDIES, studious efforts.

STYLE, title; pointed instrument used for writing on wax tablets.

SUBTLE, fine, delicate, thin; smooth, soft.

SUBTLETY (SUBTILITY), subtle device.

SUBURB, connected with loose living.

SUCCUBAE, demons in form of women.

SUCK, extract money from.

SUFFERANCE, suffering.

SUMMED, term of falconry: with full-grown plumage.

SUPER-NEGULUM, topers turned the cup bottom up when it was empty.

SUPERSTITIOUS, over-scrupulous.

SUPPLE, to make pliant.

SURBATE, make sore with walking.

SURCEASE, cease.

SUR-REVERENCE, save your reverence.

SURVISE, peruse.

SUSCITABILITY, excitability.

SUSPECT, suspicion.

SUSPEND, suspect.

SUSPENDED, held over for the present.

SUTLER, victualler.

SWAD, clown, boor.

SWATH BANDS, swaddling clothes.

SWINGE, beat.

195

TABERD, emblazoned mantle or tunic worn by knights and heralds.

TABLE(S), "pair of —," tablets, note-book.

TABOR, small drum.

TABRET, tabor.

TAFFETA, silk; "tuft-taffeta," a more costly silken fabric.

TAINT, "— a staff," break a lance at tilting in an unscientific or dishonourable manner.

TAKE IN, capture, subdue.

TAKE ME WITH YOU, let me understand you.

TAKE UP, obtain on credit, borrow.

TALENT, sum or weight of Greek currency.

TALL, stout, brave.

TANKARD-BEARERS, men employed to fetch water from the conduits.

TARLETON, celebrated comedian and jester.

TARTAROUS, like a Tartar.

TAVERN-TOKEN, "to swallow a —," get drunk.

TELL, count.

TELL-TROTH, truth-teller.

TEMPER, modify, soften.

TENDER, show regard, care for, cherish; manifest.

TENT, "take —," take heed.

TERSE, swept and polished.

196

TERTIA, "that portion of an army levied out of one particular district or division of a country" (Gifford).

TESTON, tester, coin worth 6d.

THIRDBOROUGH, constable.

THREAD, quality.

THREAVES, droves.

THREE-FARTHINGS, piece of silver current under Elizabeth.

THREE-PILED, of finest quality, exaggerated.

THRIFTILY, carefully.

THRUMS, ends of the weaver's warp; coarse yarn made from.

THUMB-RING, familiar spirits were supposed capable of being carried about in various ornaments or parts of dress.

TIBICINE, player on the tibia, or pipe.

TICK-TACK, game similar to backgammon.

TIGHTLY, promptly.

TIM, (?) expressive of a climax of nonentity.

TIMELESS, untimely, unseasonable.

TINCTURE, an essential or spiritual principle supposed by alchemists to be transfusible into material things; an imparted characteristic or tendency.

TINK, tinkle.

TIPPET, "turn —," change behaviour or way of life.

TIPSTAFF, staff tipped with metal.

TIRE, head-dress.

TIRE, feed ravenously, like a bird of prey.

TITILLATION, that which tickles the senses, as a perfume.

TOD, fox.

TOILED, worn out, harassed.

TOKEN, piece of base metal used in place of very small coin, when this was scarce.

TONNELS, nostrils.

TOP, "parish —," large top kept in villages for amusement and exercise in frosty weather when people were out of work.

TOTER, tooter, player on a wind instrument.

TOUSE, pull, rend.

TOWARD, docile, apt; on the way to; as regards; present, at hand.

TOY, whim; trick; term of contempt.

TRACT, attraction.

TRAIN, allure, entice.

TRANSITORY, transmittable.

TRANSLATE, transform.

TRAY-TRIP, game at dice (success depended on throwing a three) (Nares).

TREACHOUR (TRECHER), traitor.

TREEN, wooden.

TRENCHER, serving-man who carved or served food.

TRENDLE-TAIL, trundle-tail, curly-tailed.

TRICK (TRICKING), term of heraldry: to draw outline of coat of arms, etc., without blazoning.

TRIG, a spruce, dandified man.

TRILL, trickle.

TRILLIBUB, tripe, any worthless, trifling thing.

TRIPOLY, "come from —," able to perform feats of agility, a "jest nominal," depending on the first part of the word (Gifford).

TRITE, worn, shabby.

TRIVIA, three-faced goddess (Hecate).

TROJAN, familiar term for an equal or inferior; thief.

TROLL, sing loudly.

TROMP, trump, deceive.

TROPE, figure of speech.

TROW, think, believe, wonder.

TROWLE, troll.

TROWSES, breeches, drawers.

TRUCHMAN, interpreter.

TRUNDLE, JOHN, well-known printer.

TRUNDLE, roll, go rolling along.

TRUNDLING CHEATS, term among gipsies and beggars for carts or coaches (Gifford).

TRUNK, speaking-tube.

TRUSS, tie the tagged laces that fastened the breeches to the doublet.

TUBICINE, trumpeter.

TUCKET (Ital. toccato), introductory flourish on the trumpet.

TUITION, guardianship.

TUMBLER, a particular kind of dog so called from the mode of his hunting.

TUMBREL-SLOP, loose, baggy breeches.

TURD, excrement.

TUSK, gnash the teeth (Century Dict.).

TWIRE, peep, twinkle.

TWOPENNY ROOM, gallery.

TYRING-HOUSE, attiring-room.

ULENSPIEGEL. See Howleglass.

UMBRATILE, like or pertaining to a shadow.

UMBRE, brown dye.

UNBATED, unabated.

UNBORED, (?) excessively bored.

UNCARNATE, not fleshly, or of flesh.

UNCOUTH, strange, unusual.

UNDERTAKER, "one who undertook by his influence in the House of Commons to carry things agreeably to his Majesty's wishes" (Whalley); one who becomes surety for.

UNEQUAL, unjust.

UNEXCEPTED, no objection taken at.

UNFEARED, unaffrighted.

UNHAPPILY, unfortunately.

UNICORN'S HORN, supposed antidote to poison.

UNKIND(LY), unnatural(ly).

UNMANNED, untamed (term in falconry).

UNQUIT, undischarged.

UNREADY, undressed.

UNRUDE, rude to an extreme.

UNSEASONED, unseasonable, unripe.

UNSEELED, a hawk's eyes were "seeled" by sewing the eyelids together with fine thread.

UNTIMELY, unseasonably.

UNVALUABLE, invaluable.

UPBRAID, make a matter of reproach.

UPSEE, heavy kind of Dutch beer (Halliwell); "— Dutch," in the Dutch fashion.

UPTAILS ALL, refrain of a popular song.

URGE, allege as accomplice, instigator.

URSHIN, URCHIN, hedgehog.

USE, interest on money; part of sermon dealing with the practical application of doctrine.

USE, be in the habit of, accustomed to; put out to interest.

USQUEBAUGH, whisky.

USURE, usury.

UTTER, put in circulation, make to pass current; put forth for sale.

VAIL, bow, do homage.

VAILS, tips, gratuities.

VALL. See Vail.

VALLIES (Fr. valise), portmanteau, bag.

VAPOUR(S) (n. and v.), used affectedly, like "humour," in many senses, often very vaguely and freely ridiculed by Jonson; humour, disposition, whims, brag(ging), hector(ing), etc.

VARLET, bailiff, or serjeant-at-mace.

VAUT, vault.

VEER (naut.), pay out.

VEGETAL, vegetable; person full of life and vigour.

VELLUTE, velvet.

VELVET CUSTARD. Cf. "Taming of the Shrew," iv. 3, 82, "custard coffin," coffin being the raised crust over a pie.

VENT, vend, sell; give outlet to; scent, snuff up.

VENUE, bout (fencing term).

VERDUGO (Span.), hangman, executioner.

VERGE, "in the —," within a certain distance of the court.

VEX, agitate, torment.

VICE, the buffoon of old moralities; some kind of machinery for moving a puppet (Gifford).

VIE AND REVIE, to hazard a certain sum, and to cover it with a larger one.

VINCENT AGAINST YORK, two heralds-at-arms.

VINDICATE, avenge.

VIRGE, wand, rod.

VIRGINAL, old form of piano.

VIRTUE, valour.

VIVELY, in lifelike manner, livelily.

VIZARD, mask.

VOGUE, rumour, gossip.

VOICE, vote.

VOID, leave, quit.

VOLARY, cage, aviary.

VOLLEY, "at —," "o' the volee," at random (from a term of tennis).

VORLOFFE, furlough.

WADLOE, keeper of the Devil Tavern, where Jonson and his friends met in the 'Apollo' room (Whalley).

WAIGHTS, waits, night musicians, "band of musical watchmen" (Webster), or old form of "hautboys."

WANNION, "vengeance," "plague" (Nares).

WARD, a famous pirate.

WARD, guard in fencing.

WATCHET, pale, sky blue.

WEAL, welfare.

WEED, garment.

WEFT, waif.

WEIGHTS, "to the gold —," to every minute particular.

WELKIN, sky.

WELL-SPOKEN, of fair speech.

WELL-TORNED, turned and polished, as on a wheel.

WELT, hem, border of fur.

WHER, whether.

WHETSTONE, GEORGE, an author who lived 1544(?) to 1587(?).

WHIFF, a smoke, or drink; "taking the —," inhaling the tobacco smoke or some such accomplishment.

WHIGH-HIES, neighings, whinnyings.

WHIMSY, whim, "humour."

WHINILING, (?) whining, weakly.

WHIT, (?) a mere jot.

WHITEMEAT, food made of milk or eggs.

WICKED, bad, clumsy.

WICKER, pliant, agile.

WILDING, esp. fruit of wild apple or crab tree (Webster).

WINE, "I have the — for you," Prov.: I have the perquisites (of the office) which you are to share (Cunningham).

WINNY, "same as old word "wonne," to stay, etc." (Whalley).

WISE-WOMAN, fortune-teller.

WISH, recommend.

WISS (WUSSE), "I —," certainly, of a truth.

WITHOUT, beyond.

WITTY, cunning, ingenious, clever.

WOOD, collection, lot.

WOODCOCK, term of contempt.

WOOLSACK ("— pies"), name of tavern.

WORT, unfermented beer.

WOUNDY, great, extreme.

WREAK, revenge.

WROUGHT, wrought upon.

WUSSE, interjection. (See Wiss).

YEANLING, lamb, kid.

ZANY, an inferior clown, who attended upon the chief fool and mimicked his tricks.